The
Imagination
Box

About the author

Martyn Ford is a journalist from Hampshire, where he writes for the Bordon Herald. His first book, *It Happened to Me*, a collection of shocking true stories, was published in 2010 by Summersdale. This is his first story for young readers.

FABER & FABER has published children's books since 1929. Some of our very first publications included *Old Possum's Book of Practical Cats* by T. S. Eliot, starring the now world-famous Macavity, and *The Iron Man* by Ted Hughes. Our catalogue at the time said that 'it is by reading such books that children learn the difference between the shoddy and the genuine'. We still believe in the power of reading to transform children's lives.

The Imagination Box

Martyn Ford

FABER & FABER

First published in 2015
by Faber & Faber Limited
Bloomsbury House, 74–77 Great Russell Street
London, WC1B 3DA

Typeset by M Rules
Printed and bound by CPI Group (UK) Ltd, Croydon, CR0 4YY

A CIP record for this book is available from the British Library

ISBN 978-0-571-31165-1

6 8 10 9 8 7 5

For Inge

Prologue

'There is a box. Anything you imagine will appear inside. You have one go, one chance to create *anything* you want. What would you pick?'

The professor's voice echoed through the huge theatre. He sipped his water, breathing deliberately. For him, this was a big moment.

The audience waited quietly, hundreds of men and women – a sea of faces. There were academics, press and select members of the public, all pondering the question. A cube-shaped object, about the size of a microwave, was on the desk next to him. Although a purple velvet sheet was hiding the item, every eye in the room drifted towards it. With a deep breath, he arranged his notes on the lectern in front of him, pressed the little button on his microphone, cleared his throat and began to speak once more.

'Such a device, indeed, sounds impossible . . .'

His nerves had calmed a little; he glanced down – his hands were almost steady. The professor then took the microphone from its stand and walked confidently across the stage to the hidden desk.

'And yet, here we are,' he said, 'at the beginning. Ladies and gentlemen, it is with great pleasure that I present to you, on this humble stage, on this humble Saturday . . .' He whisked the sheet off his invention. The crowd watched on, silent now . . .

Chapter 1

One month earlier ...

The Dawn Star Hotel stood proud, even in the rain. A muggy storm swelled above the city. Tim was sitting in the hotel's huge, well-lit reception, looking out at the flurry of rush-hour workers making their way home.

It was the first day of the first week of the summer holidays. As usual, Tim was drawing. Hunched over a bird's-eye view of the umbrellas outside, he scribbled away. As he was a bit of a messy artist his picture didn't *really* resemble the rainy street scene at all. But he knew what it was meant to be and surely that's all that mattered.

'Don't you touch that sofa,' Elisa shrieked, rushing across the lobby.

She barrelled towards Tim, as if getting marks on the cushions was an emergency of giant proportions. Wetting her cloth with the bottle of spray she was clutching, she began firmly scrubbing at Tim's hands. She huffed when she saw pencil smudges on his face. Tim frowned at the smell of the cloth as it scraped up and down his cheek. This wasn't the first time she had cleaned him in the same manner she cleaned any other object. In wide-eyed horror he watched a huge drip of soapy water splash on to his masterpiece. He slammed his sketch pad shut.

'I have told you more than once about sitting here,' Elisa said.

'I was drawing the people outside.'

'The consultant is arriving shortly. The last thing he'll want to see is you sitting in reception covered in pencil lead.'

'I doubt that's the *last* thing he'll want to see,' Tim muttered. Nonetheless, he gathered his pencils and stood to leave.

'And, Tim, don't touch the cakes in the function room. They're for the staff – Donald's called a meeting.'

Tim headed out of the reception area, pushing his way through the broad oak doors into the long red-and-gold-carpeted hallway. Eyes fixed on the floor beneath, he let his imagination get the better of him. In his mind, this wasn't a carpet at all, *this* was a river of lava and the spirals were his stepping stones. Treading on the lighter parts would, therefore, result in a grizzly death. So he hopped from rock to rock, past the ground-floor rooms, each with the same door but a different, ascending bronze number.

Hang on, what's this? Delicious smells from the function room at his side slowed his pace. Chocolate? Certainly. Strawberry sponge? Without a doubt. He stopped. Tasty, fresh and, most appealingly of all, forbidden cakes; how could he possibly resist such temptation?

But wait: Tim spotted Mary, the decidedly dumpling-shaped chambermaid, at the service cupboard, preparing to do her rounds – the slight whiff of bleach and fresh towels rising from her trolley.

'Hello,' he said. She just gave a big smile in return.

Mary didn't speak much English, but she could muster enough to rat him out to Elisa if the truth about this cakey mission ever came to light. So he waited patiently on his rock, like some kind of confectionary ninja, with glowing lava licking at his feet. Mary just trampled through the bubbling magma as if it wasn't even there, pushing her trolley along and round the corner, out of sight.

Above him, mounted on the wall near the ceiling, was a CCTV camera, one of hundreds recently installed at the hotel. It gently turned its lens up and down the hall. Tim waited a moment, until it was facing away, and then approached the function-room door.

This kind of heist was a fairly typical pastime. Living where he did, at the Dawn Star, Tim had to make his own fun. After all, not really having any friends his own age (that being ten, as of last month), he spent the vast majority of his time either alone, or with adults. But that was fine; he had decided a long time ago that he preferred his own company anyway.

Paper, pencil and escaping in his own imagination – this is what Tim thought made him happy. It had never crossed his mind that he might need more.

The hotel had been Tim's home for nearly three years now, since his adoption. It sat in the centre of Glassbridge, a quaint city full of history, complete with old buildings, wonky roofs, cobblestone streets, rusted iron railings and statues of people on horseback. The place was to tourists what jam is to wasps, so the hotel was always full and the streets always busy.

Inside the function room, all the royal-red chairs were set out around a long, well-polished table. Still clutching his sketch pad under his arm and his pencils in his hand, he proceeded. There were some desks on the other side of the room, full of all kinds of food, platters of perfectly triangular sandwiches and, as expected, cake. There was also a display of the Dawn Star chocolate fudge puddings – individually presented in little glass bowls, complete with the hotel's logo on the side. Sadly, the layout was symmetrical, meaning one missing would be noticed. But then he spotted a tray of large chocolate brownies.

Like playing a game of squidgy Jenga, he picked one up from the back of the pyramid and carefully removed it without disturbing the others. Still warm, he noticed. Excellent.

It was time to leave. He turned on his heel, but stopped dead in his tracks, dropping his pad. The path was blocked by an old man wearing a rough lab coat over a white shirt, tie and a pair of thick glasses. Some kind of scientist, Tim thought. The sketchpad had fallen open on the floor; the man looked down at the umbrella picture, crouching to retrieve it.

'Indeed, yes, I could have done with one of those,' he said, passing it back.

His lab coat was wet, his shoulders peppered with raindrops. He had curled wisps of grey hair bursting from the sides of his head and his gold-framed glasses had those little half-moon magnifiers in the bottom for reading.

Tim took the book with his free hand, without uttering a word.

'They *are* umbrellas, aren't they?' the man asked. 'In your drawing?'

'Yes, they are,' Tim replied.

As he rarely drew things he saw in the real world, he was surprised to hear this picture was recognisable. In fact, the only other *real* thing he tended to sketch was his all-time favourite animal: finger monkeys – about the size of a mouse, they are so small they can wrap around your finger, hence the name. Generally, though, he did some of his best work entirely from the depths of his mind – reality offered just a dash of inspiration. Tim would conjure up distant lands and animals that, to his knowledge, had never existed. His recent creations included a rather compelling bat-dolphin-scissor-pig, and a fairly brilliant chalk and charcoal rendition of Bob the Mexican cow-snail. There was a fantastic world, endless and vibrant, enclosed inside the hard cover of his favourite sketch pad.

'Hmm, yes ... can you keep a secret?' the man whispered, bringing Tim's attention back. He peered down through thick lenses. 'I've come in here to steal a cake. Indeed.'

'Me too,' Tim said, showing the man his loot,

pleased to have a partner in crime.

'I didn't see you, and you didn't see me, right? Promise?'

'Promise.' Before he turned to leave Tim wondered what a person like this – clearly some kind of professor – was doing here. 'So, why are you at the Dawn Star?' he asked.

'Ah, now –' the man shook his head – 'let's just say, like our little theft, that it's top secret . . .'

Chapter 2

Tim's bedroom, formally room twenty, was exactly the same layout as all the guest suites in the building but looked more 'lived in', with considerably more mess. Sitting cross-legged on the end of his bed, he put the final touches on his drawing, turning Elisa's accidental watermark into a puddle on the pavement.

The phone on his bedside cabinet rang. It was Elisa, calling him for dinner. She often contacted him on the hotel's internal system. This made Tim feel even more like a guest and less like her son. Elisa and Chris Green, who ran the Dawn Star, had adopted him a week or two before they moved in. At the time it was a dream come true for them, as Elisa had wanted to run a hotel since she was little. This confused Tim because she never seemed to be happy here – in fact just the opposite. She was constantly anxious, spending much of her time upset about money, about how hard things were or about how she didn't have time for any of Tim's nonsense, 'nonsense' being virtually anything Tim said or did. This worked out quite nicely as he'd much rather sit by himself in some corner somewhere than be forced to spend time with Elisa.

As for Chris, well, Tim liked him a lot but they were very rarely together as he spent most of his time away on business. Working for some internet company, he was regularly jetting around the world, to sell or buy or look at or talk about . . . stuff. But when he was there, he was always asking what Tim was up to and he *always* cared about the answer. It was funny to think that Chris would be the ideal parent if he was there more and Elisa would be the ideal parent if she was there less.

And – although Tim knew the adoption was a permanent arrangement, that they had indeed signed documents meaning they were his legal guardians in every sense – he still couldn't help feeling as though they might not be his parents forever. Sooner or later, he suspected, he'd be thrown back into one of the countless institutions through which he'd passed.

More than anything, though, Tim found the hotel a rather dull place, despite the corridor of lava. Even a brother or sister might brighten things up.

'I'm too busy for children,' Elisa sighed when he suggested that. She followed it with a guilty frown as, of course, Tim knew this to be all too true.

Chris and Elisa occupied what used to be the biggest room in the hotel, but which had been converted into living quarters when they took over. Here they'd meet as a 'family' to enjoy a quiet and generally tense meal together.

That night was no different. Elisa moaned for a while about the fact that the hotel's head chef was leaving, and complained about how expensive things were getting, particularly the new CCTV cameras that she was having installed, and the added costs of the consultant she'd hired. She also told Tim that an 'important guest' was staying in room nineteen, opposite his bedroom, so he should be quiet.

Chris had cooked too, which meant the food was questionable. The sausages looked like coal and the mash was . . . well, Tim couldn't be sure if it even was potato. He much preferred it when Elisa cooked, even if it created extra tension.

After dinner Tim returned to his bedroom and, the moment he closed the door, he heard some commotion in the hallway. Using his swivel chair, which he knelt on after rolling it across his carpet, he looked through the peephole. He spotted a man outside room nineteen carrying a huge cardboard box – it was the scientist, his cake-thief friend, and clearly the person Elisa had mentioned. Tim was intrigued. The old man was fumbling with the lock, whilst balancing the giant box with his other hand. It looked far too heavy for him and he seemed all the more comical through the peephole – distorted and stretched.

'Come on, you slippery, wiggly little . . .' the old man mumbled. The key tumbled from his hand.

Tim clambered off his chair and opened his door.

'Would you like some help with that?' he asked.

The man turned slowly, straining his neck.

He smiled as best he could, the weight of the box visible on his face.

'Ah, hello. Indeed, yes, if you could retrieve the key, there, on the floor.' He pointed with a tilt of his head and a madman's wink. Tim crouched and picked it up.

'Now, yes,' he continued, 'if you could throw it into my mouth I think I might be able to unlock the door with my teeth ...' Leaning forwards, he held his lips open and waited.

'Um, I could ... just open the door for you?'

'Hmm, no ... wait ... Yes! Much better idea. Let's do that.'

After Tim had let him in, the man carefully placed the cardboard box on the floor and stood up straight with a groan. 'Oh, oh, that's better ... Nice to get my back upright again. It's you, isn't it? It is.' He squinted through his specs.

'It's me?'

'You, yes, indeed, the boy. I hope you kept your promise and didn't tell anyone about ...'

'I didn't. Although Elisa saw chocolate on my face, so *I* was rumbled.' All hell had broken loose over dinner. Elisa said Tim never did as he was told and never listened to what she said … or something like that.

'Oh yes, of course … wait … Elisa?' he frowned.

'She's the owner, the manager,' Tim said.

'The manager of the brownies? What a fine job.'

'No,' Tim laughed. 'She's the manager of the hotel. My adoptive mother – she takes care of me. Well, she feeds me and provides me with a room to sleep in …'

'Oh yes, yes. I know Elisa. I am glad you kept your promise. A promise between friends … oh my, it is not to be broken. I am George Eisenstone,' he said, extending his arm to Tim.

'Timothy Hart.'

They shook hands.

'Elisa said I shouldn't disturb you,' Tim added, turning to leave.

'Ah, no, no,' he smiled. 'This is my room, I have paid no small sum to stay here. Indeed. It is up to me who comes and goes. Besides, you, well, helped me with my box.'

'She told me not to annoy you.'

'No doubt she told you not to steal a cake too. You are not annoying me, young man. No, no.' Eisenstone sat on the bed, removed his glasses and began cleaning them with a small yellow square of soft material.

The only thing as deep as Tim's imagination was his curiosity. 'So . . . what's in the box?' he asked.

Eisenstone glanced over his shoulder. 'In there is my work. It is very important.'

The vague answers were simply making him more excited. 'And what, exactly, is that?'

'Secrets.' The professor smiled. 'At any rate, I fear it won't be terribly interesting. My work isn't . . . it isn't finished. Now . . .' Eisenstone pulled a small silver watch from his top pocket to check the time. 'I must go. I have arrangements.'

'OK.'

'It was nice to meet you,' he said, standing.

On the way out Tim peered over for one last quick glance. He struggled with his inquisitive nature at the best of times, but a big mysterious box filled solely with secrets? This was some kind of torture.

The moment he returned to his room, he knelt back

on top of his swivel chair and watched the professor leave. This man *was* intriguing, Tim concluded, still staring through the peephole. Out of the ordinary, and certainly worth investigating—

Hang on.

A strip of natural light escaped into the hall from room nineteen. The door was open, only a slither, but open nonetheless. Professor Eisenstone must have assumed the first click meant it was locked. In actual fact these old doors needed quite a tug to close completely.

Interesting . . .

Again, Tim left his bedroom and stood for a moment alone in the corridor, biting his thumbnail as he evaluated the temptation.

Could he?

He couldn't. It wouldn't be right.

But . . . maybe . . . maybe just a quick peek. What's the worst that could happen?

So he pushed the door open a tiny amount and sneaked a look inside the room. The cardboard box was on the bed, on its side. It was empty.

He stopped for a moment and considered turning back. If Professor Eisenstone returned he'd be angry – he might even tell Elisa. But maybe just a little further, he thought.

On the floor, he saw some wires. Red, white, green, blue and striped ones all tangled and bunched together with elastic bands. His gaze followed the cables to a large silver contraption sitting on top of the wooden chest of drawers next to the bed. It looked like a microwave, only ... different. There were exposed circuit boards and a forest of complicated-looking buttons and settings on top. Whatever it was it looked homemade and unfinished. A small hatch on the top of the box caught Tim's eye. He slid a metal lock, like one from a bathroom, and lifted the lid. The machine was hollow, empty. What does this thing do, Tim silently wondered.

Below him, resting on the carpet, was what looked like a very unusual hat plugged into the box. Before Tim could stop himself, the helmet had found its way on to *his* head.

It felt heavy and uncomfortable as he continued

inspecting the main part of the machine. On the top right-hand side was one button that stood out. It had nothing written on it but it was big, circular and green – green being the universal colour for 'Go', and circles, well, they're just an all-round nice shape.

Then, with no conscious thought, Tim's hand moved forward and pressed the button.

Whoops.

There was a quiet beep when he pulled his arm away. He waited a second, watching a small blue light flash on the top of the device, but nothing happened.

Tim sighed, disappointed to have come this far and still be no closer to knowing what this thing was. The clock on the wall gently ticked. With his tongue he picked at his teeth, briefly recalling Chris's recent attempt at dinner. Swallowing, he winced at the taste, thinking of those terrible, crunchy, burnt-black sausages, they were just—

With another, louder beep the box lit up and started vibrating on the chest of drawers. Tim stepped back, alarmed. It groaned, shook and clacked an orchestra of sounds. Quickly, he yanked the hat-thing off his head and dropped it on the floor, taking another step away. Buzzing and shuffling and clattering around on top of the wood, it seemed alive. For a good twenty seconds it noisily did *something*.

Eventually, the machine stuttered and hummed slowly to silence, like a vacuum cleaner whirring down. All the lights faded but the tiny blue bulb continued to flash.

Pausing to make sure the odd cube had definitely finished whatever it was it was doing, he approached. It sat there peacefully, a tiny lick of steam escaping from a vent at the back. There was a vague smell, like his computer's fan. A dusty, plastic, electric odour.

Tim put his hand on the little hatch on top, feeling that it was warm, and began to open—

'TIMOTHY HART!' screamed a voice.

He swung round, like a rabbit in headlights, to see Elisa in the doorway.

Back in his bedroom, the shouting had been rumbling in the background for some time.

'No drawing for a week,' Elisa announced – this

caught his attention. 'There's nothing else I can do to punish you, Tim. I can't ground you – you've not got any friends.' Her eyes darted to the ground as she turned away. Tim suspected she regretted saying that but it didn't slow her collecting his drawing stuff. She even yanked all the paper out of the printer. Finally, she'd lost it.

'Elisa, I wouldn't dream of criticising your disciplinary techniques,' he began cautiously. 'I *completely* understand why you're doing this, I do get it. But you're meant to encourage children's creativity – stopping me from drawing is probably not a good idea.'

He wasn't as bothered as he should have been about this – he had back-up pencils and paper dotted all over the place.

'Of course *you* don't think it's a good idea, that's the point of a punishment.'

She finished gathering up his things, tossed them into a bin liner, then opened the door. Across the hall Tim saw the professor arriving at his room.

'Ah,' Elisa said. 'Mr Eisenstone, just the man I

want to speak to. Tim, come here and say sorry this instant.'

After a couple of false starts, Tim tentatively explained.

'Hmm,' Eisenstone thought for a moment. 'Apology accepted.'

'Upstairs, now,' Elisa said. 'You can do *all* the washing-up today.'

Truthfully, Tim *was* sorry. Not because he broke the rules, but because he had betrayed the professor's trust. However, soon it simply wouldn't matter as, unbeknown to Tim, something that would change the world forever was waiting for Eisenstone in room nineteen.

Chapter 3

As part of his punishment for trespassing in Eisenstone's room, Tim was forced to wash and dry a frankly absurd amount of plates, pots and pans in Chris and Elisa's living quarters. When he was finished, he returned straight to his bedroom where, on the carpet, a small piece of paper had been slipped under his door.

Picking it up, he unfolded it to read, 'Tim, come and see me when you get this note. George Eisenstone.'

It was signed with the most magnificent signature he had ever seen. It covered much of the small, lined sheet. The 'G' on George spiralled wildly and whipped across to the top of the 'E' in Eisenstone.

Wondering why he'd been summoned, Tim knocked on room nineteen's thick wooden door.

The professor let him in. 'Sit down, Tim,' he said, perching on the corner of his bed and gesturing at a chair in the corner.

It was hard to judge his mood – he didn't *seem* particularly angry but, as Tim took a seat, he felt the need to apologise all over again.

'I'm really, really sorry,' he said. 'I just saw that your door was—'

'Tim, Tim, it's fine, I don't mind. In your shoes I would have done the same. Indeed. Curiosity is ... well ... a good thing; don't listen when people tell you it isn't.'

'OK.' Tim was a little confused.

'But, buttery but, but, but, let me ask you something, and it's important you're honest ... *what* were you thinking when you pressed the button?' He pointed at the device in the corner. Tim had been making a special effort not to look at it.

'I am really sorry. I don't know what came over me.' Tim's voice was jittery – he didn't like being told off (apart from by Elisa – hc sort of enjoyed that in a weird way).

'No, no. Tim. No. You misunderstand. I am asking you what you were thinking about. Tell me, literally, indeed, *what* you were thinking the moment you pressed that button ... you were wearing the reader, yes?'

'The reader?' Tim asked.

'The reader. The hat thingy. The ... thing ... you put on your head.'

'I ...' Tim looked at the floor, ashamed.

'Yes.' Eisenstone leant forward, eager for the information.

'I ... I was thinking. I don't know ...' Tim searched his brain – he closed his eyes to remember. 'I thought about how silly I looked. I saw myself in the mirror. The hat, helmet, reader thing, it was too big for me. I was scared Elisa would come in. I was scared *you* would come in. But I pressed the button and then waited and there was a long pause ... I thought about ... about ... I looked at the clock ... then I, I picked some food out of my teeth.'

'Yes?!' Eisenstone yelled, overly excited, leaning even closer. 'And what did you think?!'

'It was, um, I thought about dinner. I thought about how bad a cook Chris is.'

'YES! Why? What's wrong with his cooking?'

Tim opened his eyes. 'Everything. I mean, don't get me wrong, Chris is a great guy but his food is bordering on illegal. If Social Services came by, I'd hide it. He has this habit of making the most disgusting, horrid, hard, dry, black, burnt-to-a-crisp—'

'Let me guess,' Eisenstone whispered, lifting his brow. 'Sausages?'

'Yes,' Tim replied in surprise.

The professor's face lit up as he stood, clapping his hands. He grabbed Tim by the shoulders.

'This is amazing!' he yelled, shaking him. 'Indeed. Do you know what this means?'

'I really don't.'

Excitement had possessed Eisenstone. He began to pace, mumbling to himself. Pointing to the ceiling, he stopped and turned to Tim.

'You have no idea how incredible you are, do you?'

'I've had my suspicions.' Tim wasn't sure what the professor was banging on about, but smiled nonetheless.

'What you've done is . . .' Eisenstone looked around the room for the right words. 'Brilliant!' He clenched his fists. 'You're a genius, my boy. A genius. Although, it must be secret. For now. But then when it's written up and complete. Patents and studies all done. My word. When it's all complete. The potential. The implications!'

'Professor Eisenstone,' Tim said, calmly, 'what is so exciting?'

'I'll *show* you!'

The contraption was open and on the side next to it was a shoebox, from which Eisenstone removed something, before flicking the cardboard lid across the room. He hurried back and stood in front of Tim clutching a sandwich bag.

'Hold out your hand,' he said.

Tim did as he was told, still seated and still frankly nervous about all this unexplained joy. A shrivelled-up sausage, wrapped in plastic, dropped into Tim's palm.

The professor nodded manically, biting his fist in anticipation. 'It's a sausage!' he sang.

'Yes,' Tim said, frowning. 'A burnt one.'

It had all got a bit odd and Tim was starting to think Eisenstone might actually be mad, just a mentally ill old man. Sad, really. Maybe he'd just escaped from somewhere. Maybe he was the Professor of Crayon Digestion at the University of Loopyville.

'I've run tests,' Eisenstone continued. 'It's made of pork, a few herbs and spices. Traces of salt, of water – believe it or not, all the ingredients you'd need to make a sausage.' The professor grabbed Tim again and knelt, staring intensely. 'All the ingredients.'

'Forgive me, again, but what on earth is so amazing about a sausage?'

'Nothing. Absolutely nothing. But a sausage you've made appear, using only your mind and my device. Indeed, *that*, my boy, is amazing.'

'I see.' Tim glanced to the door. 'Wait, hang on. That sausage was in your machine ... thing? But I checked inside before I did anything. It was empty ...'

'Yes, it *was*. That's the whole point.'

'What *is* that box?' he whispered.

Arms out, flapping like wings, Eisenstone danced to the contraption where he stood proudly.

'This, young Timothy, is an atomic arrangement vessel.' He held his hands out and widened his eyes, as though Tim was meant to understand.

'A whaty what what?'

'And, because of you, it actually works.'

'What does an atom … arrangement … thing actually do?'

'Ah!' Eisenstone turned to the device. 'A fine question indeed. Well … essentially, what happens is millions of airborne nanomachines equipped with primitive artificial intelligence construct any item one can imagine … with certain restraints. Oh yes. Quite.'

'Right,' Tim said, raising an eyebrow.

'You see, I am a theoretical particle physicist. Yes. Yes. Energy, motion, space and time.' He clicked his fingers. 'And *this* is my invention. I call it the thought-directed atomic construction device. Or a TDACD for short …'

'So, it . . . it reads your thoughts and then makes . . . *constructs* whatever you imagine?'

'Precisely.'

'Hang on,' Tim added. 'If I imagined, say, a pencil with this hat . . . helmet—'

'Reader.'

'With this reader thing on my head, and pressed the button, you're telling me a pencil would appear inside?'

'Tim,' Eisenstone said, nodding, 'that's *exactly* what I'm telling you.'

'Wow.'

'Although, honestly, no one has yet been able to successfully make an object. Even tiny ones, a few atoms big, have been a struggle. It's the signals . . . from the brain . . . electromagnetic . . . I mean . . .' He seemed to wince at how complicated it was. 'To have the clarity of thought you have . . . And something so complex. A sausage! Cooked to imperfection. It's all been theory up until you came along.'

'Hmm.' Tim nodded, wandering over. 'Can I?' he

asked with his hand above the box, keen to inspect it again, now he knew its potential.

'Go ahead.'

Lifting the lid, Tim saw that little electronic components lined the inside. Excitement bubbled as his mind came alive with all the possible things he could conjure.

'And what did you say you call it?' he asked.

'A thought-directed atomic construction device. Indeed,' Eisenstone tilted his head and exhaled. 'TDACD.'

'You should have a shorter name for it,' Tim said, holding the reader in his hands.

'Hmm. I've done brainstorms, you know, whiteboards, spider-grams, the works. The name is . . . it's a winner.'

'Nah. Call it . . .' Tim said, thinking. 'Call it . . . the imagination box.'

Chapter 4

Tim, of course, had wanted to start imagining things straightaway, but the professor insisted on waiting until they were both in his lab – a 'secure, private and scientific' environment.

The following day, after a short drive across Glassbridge, Eisenstone and Tim arrived at what looked like an old industrial estate. However, one brand-new building, clad in modern pine and lightly tinted glass, stood out from all the rest. This was the professor's place of work and Tim was keen to get inside and try the imagination box again – properly this time.

That morning the professor had had a quick chat with Elisa, and told her he needed Tim to help with a study at his laboratory. Worrying that she might see this as an opportunity for further punishment for trespassing in room nineteen, Tim tried not to show his excitement at the prospect. Luckily, she didn't seem to mind – her thoughts were clearly elsewhere. She was tied up chatting to Donald Pinkman, the hotel's new consultant, whom she'd hired to make things run 'more smoothly'.

Inside the large building, Eisenstone seemed to relax. They passed through countless corridors and five checkpoints, all of which required him to show ID and to swipe a card. It gave Tim the sense that a lot of important and groundbreaking work must go on in this sprawling complex.

During the car ride there, Tim had stared out of the window and wondered aloud why – if it was so important the box remained a secret – the professor was keeping it in the hotel.

'There must be more suitable places,' he said. 'I mean, I got my hands on it.'

'As fate would have it, indeed.'

Besides Tim's trespass, the Dawn Star Hotel was,

the professor had explained, 'perhaps the most secure place of all'.

'Burglar alarms, modern CCTV, both private *and* public,' he had said. 'It is maybe the safest place for me, and for the invention. But, indeed, perhaps I've become too comfortable, complacent, letting down my guard. At any rate, as lovely as the establishment is, I assure you, Tim, this is no holiday for me.'

After what seemed a mile walking down long corridors, they arrived at a final door, which hissed open following a card swipe. Gradually, one bulb after another flickered on until the room was covered in clean white light.

Tim had seen spaces like this in countless sci-fi films, but this one was better, neater and minimalist.

'Ah, yes, you can tell I've not been here for a while,' Eisenstone said. 'Look how tidy it is . . .'

While he unpacked and prepared, Tim tried to wait patiently near the door, but the temptation to go off exploring grew unbearable. About eleven seconds later, he ventured deeper into the lab.

There was the usual kind of equipment, test tubes

and beakers, and also a number of gadgets and electronic bits and pieces, all housed on pedestals and in transparent boxes, like exhibits in a museum. As he threaded his way through the room, running his fingers along the desks – making two legs out of his index and middle – he guessed that most of the items he saw were in some way related to the imagination box. The whole place seemed dedicated to it – years and years of groundbreaking work was on display.

He arrived at a workstation with a wide computer screen, surrounded by notes and photos. Sunlight drew horizontal lines across the wood, striped by the slats on the window's blind. Specs of dust danced, only visible in the glowing layers of air.

'Who is this?' Tim asked, holding up a framed picture of a girl around his age.

'Ah, quite. That is Dee, my granddaughter,' Eisenstone said, walking over to him. 'She's about your age – eleven come March. She's in my garden, see.' He tapped on the glass.

Dee was wearing a red polka-dot dress and standing

amongst a number of exotic-looking flowers, in front of an autumn sunset. She had Professor Eisenstone's ever-so-slightly manic smile.

'You have a nice garden.'

'Yes, quite.'

'Is it far away?'

'My garden?' Eisenstone said. 'No, it's near Winter Church. But as I said before, my home isn't a great place to be at the moment . . . certainly not in light of recent breakthroughs. Too dangerous.'

'Dangerous?' Tim frowned.

'Oh yes. There are forces afoot that would move heaven and earth for this prototype, indeed.' He placed the frame back on the desk, proudly straightening it. 'And, yes, Dee's a good girl, very clever. She's an all-right artist like you. Creative does seem to be the default setting for children . . .'

'So, do you reckon she could use the box?' Tim asked. 'Has she tried?'

'I . . . I wouldn't feel comfortable testing it on her,' Eisenstone said.

'Why?'

'It's . . . complicated. I wouldn't have let you try it either, had you not done so by yourself.'

The imagination box was set on a table; next to it was a laptop with a microphone plugged in, a digital camcorder and two stools, awaiting Tim and Eisenstone. They both sat.

'OK, now, yes, right, let's—' A phone on the wall began to ring. 'Quite perfect timing,' the professor sighed. 'Hello,' he said into the handset as he tugged at the curly wire.

Tim couldn't hear who was on the other end or what they said, but Eisenstone's face went a peculiar shade of grey as his smile disappeared.

'OK,' he said. 'Bring him down.'

He returned to the table and perched on the stool.

'Tim, we'll have to carry on in a little bit. I have an important guest. A policeman.'

A few minutes later, the door buzzed, hissed and clunked open and a security guard Tim had seen earlier entered. He was followed by a chubby man, wearing a long, light brown coat, with a shirt and tie underneath.

Eisenstone thanked the guard, who departed, leaving the guest behind.

'George,' the large man said, shaking hands.

'Inspector Kane,' the professor replied.

They walked into the corner and spoke in hushed voices – Tim couldn't hear what was being said. The policeman had short brown hair, stubble and tired-looking eyes. At one point he got something from his pocket and Tim spotted the corner of a bronze-coloured badge, mounted on leather, holstered on his belt.

As they spoke, Inspector Kane looked over, made eye contact and smiled warmly. Tim snapped his gaze on to the laptop in front of him in an effort to pretend he wasn't staring.

Their chat ended and the security guard returned and escorted the policeman out of the building.

'Yes, yes, sorry about that,' Eisenstone said, returning to his seat.

'Was it . . . bad news?' Tim asked, unable to resist being nosy.

'No. Well, yes and no. As I said, Inspector Kane is

a policeman. You see, my briefcase was stolen from me a few weeks ago and he's following up with some leads. All my notes, my work, all gone. Goney gone gone. It was taken from my home and I, for one, don't believe it was opportunistic.'

'What do you mean?'

'I ...' Eisenstone seemed suddenly saddened. He sighed and cringed at a memory. 'It's complex, but ... I ... you see, I had an old friend, Professor Whitelock ... We shared much of our career together, we were ... academic partners. Yes. For years we'd been working on this very thing, on an atomic constructor, an imagination box. We were making real progress. But a couple of months ago he ... sadly, he died.'

'Oh ...' Tim was surprised to hear the invention had a rocky history – he expected such a device to have come about in a fairy-tale kind of way – spark of inspiration, bit of computer stuff, soldering, some Sellotape, done.

'Yes. Well, Whitelock went a bit ... shall we say ... odd. They say there's a fine line between genius and madness. Well, Professor Whitelock was certainly a genius, but it seemed he also crossed the line. He became ill, he . . . he lost his mind.'

'Lost his mind? Ketchup on cornflakes or . . .?'

'Worse. You see, we drifted apart and I hadn't heard from him for a fair while . . . and then there was an incident. A fire at his laboratory. He was killed, maybe murdered, and much of his . . . much of *our* work was lost. True enough, we'd not been close towards the end . . . but I still miss him every day. Tragically he'd just got married too. Very sad times indeed. The point is, although it has never been proven, I don't think his death was an accident.'

'Someone started the fire deliberately?'

'I suspect so.'

'Why?' Tim had heard of academic rivals, but arson . . . murder? This seemed all together more serious.

'I feel it was to cover up a theft. For many years he'd been working on a teleporter.'

'Really?' What other incredible gadgets was the professor involved with, Tim wondered.

'Yes, the technology, you understand, is not dissimilar from the imagination box. To teleport something you must first break it down, in essence destroy it, and then recreate it at another location. Rumour had it that he'd successfully teleported a live owl.'

'Wow.'

'Indeed. And, well, very few people knew what he was up to, so when the police discovered his lab burned down – his work destroyed – they wouldn't have been looking for a missing teleporter. In fact, they ignored it entirely. I tried to tell them that it was stolen, but my words fell on deaf ears – indeed, I'm not sure they ever really believed me.'

'So someone killed him, just to steal his teleporter?'

Eisenstone exhaled with a shrug. 'I just can't be sure. I might be paranoid – it might be silly of me to seek refuge in the Dawn Star. But I've been burgled twice now, and both times my notes have been taken. I just have this terrible feeling that whoever targeted Whitelock might be targeting me.'

Now Tim could see real worry in the professor's eyes

and had a sudden pang of fear himself, wondering if he too was in any kind of danger. However, as he watched Eisenstone prepare the imagination box for testing, there was no denying that this was also alluring.

'Anyway, enough about all that – we've got work to do, yes?' The professor pulled a large notepad from his satchel and began patting himself down.

'Now, now, Tim, you don't happen to have a pencil on you?'

'Always,' Tim replied, pulling a tiny red pencil from his shirt pocket. 'I don't go anywhere without one.'

'Oh yes, I'm the same with this,' Eisenstone replied, sliding his silver watch out of his pocket and placing it on the desk between them.

'It's nice.' Tim picked it up and looked on the back – engraved there were the letters 'PE'. He ran his finger across the initials, feeling the depth of the carving.

'Peter Eisenstone was my father. Yes. He gave me this when I was about your age. Or a bit younger. Or older. Indeed. That watch has never left my side. I don't go anywhere without it.'

'I need a watch,' Tim said, sliding it back across the wood.

'Maybe *your* father will—' Eisenstone realised what he was saying and stopped himself. 'Sorry.'

'It's fine. Maybe I'll make one in the machine,' Tim laughed.

The professor paused, fiddling with the corner of his notepad. His eyes drifted away and then swept back to Tim.

'What happened to your parents?' he said, cautiously. 'If you don't mind me asking?'

Surprised by the question – people rarely asked – Tim shuffled in his seat. 'Um … well … my mother died when I was a baby and then my father disappeared. I lived with some people and then some others and then some others and now Chris and Elisa. Strange, isn't it?'

'Oh yes, my yes, very.'

'Sometimes people just disappear and never return. Really, it happens a lot. Look it up. Hundreds of people go missing every year, and don't come back. I sometimes wonder where he is, and then I realise if he's still alive he doesn't want to be found, and if he's dead, he can't be. So there's no point in me worrying about it.'

Eisenstone slowly nodded. He seemed to respect Tim's attitude. 'You really do remind me of Dee,' he said, moving his notepad to one side. 'Righto. Now we go to the fun bit. The bit with all the fun. Let's start with a marble, Tim. Indeed, can you do that?'

The professor placed the reader on Tim's head, adjusted some wiring and then pressed the button.

'Just as before,' he said. 'Just imagine it.'

Scrunching his face, Tim closed his eyes, focusing hard on keeping his mind clear of other thoughts, ignoring all sounds, just thinking about marbles.

But nothing happened.

He looked around, bewildered. Eisenstone pouted, frowning a little. Again, Tim covered his eyes and tried – really concentrating now. His mind took a few moments to completely craft the image a second time and then, finally, like a key turning in a lock, the infinite variations he *could* have imagined slipped away and a picture of a perfect glass sphere settled. A swirl of blue spiralled through the core and a spectacular gloss rolled across the surface.

The machine rumbled into life, buzzing and clunking, hissing and vibrating as it did its constructing. They watched the small blue light on top of the imagination box return to flashing – signalling completion. Then the professor slid the lock open and pulled the lid back, while Tim tensely chewed his thumb.

What if there was nothing in there at all? What if he couldn't do it a second time? He found himself holding his breath as Eisenstone stared silently into the box.

Please let it work.

Slowly the professor slipped back on to his stool, a single tear falling from his cheek.

'Are you OK?' Tim asked, concerned. *It hadn't worked.*

'Tim ...' Eisenstone said, 'this is the happiest moment of my life. This *is* very good indeed.' He stood and turned away – clearly overwhelmed by the moment. The old man's shoulders lifted a little up and down. At first Tim thought he was crying, but then he heard rising laughter.

With a knee on the desk, Tim leant over to look. Sure enough, a marble rolled around at the bottom of the box, resting in the corner of the metal interior. He'd done it.

At around five, Eisenstone drove them back to the hotel. They pulled into the car park behind the building, next to the alleyway leading to the back of the kitchen. From here Tim could see his bedroom window. Steam rose out from a vent and a slight smell of dinner filled the car park.

'Can I ask you one more favour, Tim?' Eisenstone said in a serious tone.

'Yes.'

'Please, please, don't tell anyone specifically what we've been doing. Not even Chris or Elisa. It's important. Very, very.'

'Um … OK.' Tim had no trouble with white lies when it came to Elisa – they were his bread and butter.

Lying to Chris was never as easy, but he'd respect Eisenstone's wishes – despite the temptation.

'Soon, soon, soon, when it's all put together and we know it works—'

'It does work.'

'It's . . . it's early days still. This is a big deal, Tim. This will change . . . everything. Once we understand the technology a bit better, we can ensure it is safe. In the right hands, this could be a revolutionary machine – in the wrong hands, well, it could be catastrophic.'

Chapter 5

'So I *can* make, say . . . a spoon?'

'Yes.'

'Could I make . . . a cow?'

'No. Yes. Well . . . potentially, yes, a small one. Or in a bigger machine, it's possible you could make a cow. It's complex, but yes, essentially, yes. Not in this prototype of course.'

It was day two of their experimenting at the lab. Eisenstone had just made them both a hot chocolate and was attempting to explain the physical nature of the universe. He said he wanted Tim to understand the science behind the imagination box before they made the next item. There were also plans to test Tim's brain – to take various readings.

'Matter. Indeed. It's a tricky concept to get your head around,' Eisenstone said. 'You see, me, you, everyone, everything, we're made of stuff. Made of bits of stuff. That stuff was made in the stars a long time ago and it has just been arranged in lots of different ways. Like a supermarket that has eggs, flour and sugar inside. Everything you need to make a cake. Humans, well we're made mostly of water, which is made of oxygen and hydrogen. Then there is some carbon, calcium, nitrogen and a few other bits and pieces. The point is, it's *stuff*. Everything is. Think of the world like that and well, indeed, it's remarkably wonderful.'

'I see,' Tim replied, nodding, looking briefly at his own hand. He glanced at the device, wondering silently what he would make if he was given a free go. There were countless options.

Eisenstone stood and took his hot chocolate over to his other desk. He started tapping away on the computer with his back to Tim, who was still on the bench with the imagination box in front of him. Annoyingly, the professor was in no rush to make things and was forcing Tim to be patient while he typed up endless notes. After all, he'd been working on this gadget for years. However Tim was growing impatient. Half of him wanted to conduct himself like a scientist, going slowly one step at a time, recording findings as he went. La, la, la. But he also just wanted to get that reader on and see what he could make. And, more importantly, see what he *couldn't* make.

'How about a potato?' Tim asked, with a shrug.

'Yes, even easier than a cow.'

'A jar of … jam?'

'Yes.'

'A jar of … salad cream?'

'Yes.'

'A jar of … anger.'

'Yes. Wait … no. No.'

'Not a jar of anger?'

'Nothing abstract. I think, no. Anything concrete. A rock, yes. A shoelace, yes. Happiness, no. Ambition, no, I don't presume so. These are not solid, tangible things. I would deduce from my research, indeed, that you could make a custard-flavoured belt, for instance, or a sock filled with rainbow-coloured tea leaves, but try and make a bubble of maybe, or an egg cup filled with lies and you'll run into trouble. Indeed, anything you could pick up . . .'

'*Any*thing?'

'Well. No. Weightless lead or hot ice, these are not possible. It mustn't conflict with the laws of physics. It can't be . . . it can't be *impossible*.'

Tim was fiddling idly with the helmet, entangling his fingers in the wire. 'I guess that depends on the definition of the word.'

'Oh yes, lovely, yes, I admire your thinking,' Eisenstone said, turning his body on his stool. 'There is something quite excellent about the way your mind works. I guess it's only with age we gain restrictions. Yes, quite poetic, isn't it.'

'What if the limits were just our imagination?' Tim had something in mind.

'Now, now, I hate to disappoint you, Tim, but the imagination box isn't magic – it does have restrictions. Remember, what it does is simply build things, like if you made a house from Lego. Except it uses atoms instead.'

Tim looked over to Eisenstone, who was still facing away, absorbed in his computer. 'I could make anything out of Lego ... if I had enough bricks,' he said, placing the reader on his head.

Lifting a finger, he thought of the one thing he'd always wanted, one thing he'd dreamed of during those long afternoons, one thing he'd sketched time and time again. Wearing the metal helmet, he visualised his next creation, reached out and pressed the button.

The beep, the clunk, the whizzing and the machine was once again alive. Eisenstone shut his laptop and turned to look.

'Oh, Tim, you just couldn't wait, could you?' he said over the noise.

It settled down, with a puff of steam and the now-familiar blue light, Tim's creation inside.

'What have you made?' Eisenstone asked with a half smile.

Without another word, Tim leant over, clunked the lock and gasped as he lifted the lid.

A tiny monkey, no larger than a mouse, leapt out on to the edge of the box.

53

'It worked!' Tim yelled with joy.

The creature looked up at them, glancing from one to the other frantically as it took in its surroundings. It had brown fur with a striped tail and huge, cautious eyes. It hopped fluidly, like a squirrel, along the top of the machine to one corner where it peered down, before shuffling back to its original spot. They both watched the incredible animal in absolute amazement.

'I call him ... Phillip, or Phil. Phil the finger monkey,' Tim said, leaning in for a closer look. 'Seems a reasonable name.'

Cautiously, the creature reached up and touched his nose with one of its absurdly small hands. With a giggle, Tim flinched back and it scurried away a little on the lid. Then, tentatively, it returned to the edge, inspecting Tim's face.

After a moment of quiet contemplation of its creator, the finger monkey relaxed, glanced around at the space near the box and then leapt on to the desk. It went straight for Tim's hot chocolate, fishing out a marshmallow and experimentally nibbling on the corner. Eisenstone and Tim remained transfixed as it sat merrily devouring the squishy sweet.

'It is … utterly *incredible*, Tim.' Eisenstone was clearly baffled. 'An organism. So complicated, so perfect. It's intelligent, it's … I … *Indeed* … I never even considered that *this* machine could be used to make living creatures. To create *life*.'

The tiny animal stopped to look directly into the professor's eyes, which stared back adoringly, large behind lenses.

'Hello, little monkey.' Eisenstone said, leaning closer.

'Hello?' Phil replied, clearly.

Tim's eyes and mouth widened in unison. It had worked.

Arms flopping by his side, the professor stood, knocking his stool back on to the floor.

'Pardon?' he said, turning his neck as if he was scared of the answer.

'I said … ah, hello,' Phil replied, in an elegantly posh voice, just as Tim had imagined.

Eisenstone pulled his glasses from his face,

dropping them on the desk, then rubbed his forehead, placing his other palm on the table next to Phil. Tim looked between them, frankly enjoying the professor's reaction.

'You . . . you can . . . no. You can't . . . but you can,' Eisenstone was flabbergasted. 'You can talk. Indeed you seem to be able to talk. But you surely . . . No.'

'It certainly seems so,' Phil replied with a smile. He scurried back to the marshmallow. 'Now, not another word from me until you chaps explain what this extravagantly beautiful thing is?'

The monkey dragged the sweet along the desk; it was half his size so it seemed to be a little bit of a struggle.

'It's a marshmallow,' Tim said. He remembered the daydreams he'd had, time and time again, when he imagined what it might be like to have the best pet on earth, but he didn't dare think it would be *this* good.

'Well, it is delicious, and I thank you for it.'

'Care to try the hot chocolate?' Tim asked, quickly accepting that Phil could talk. He was surprised, sure, but deep down he had expected it to work. If Tim had faith in *anyone* it was himself.

'May I?' Phil said, turning his tiny head back to the cup.

After dipping his little finger in the hot chocolate, Tim dangled a drop above Phil.

'That is most amazing. Can you acquire more?' he asked, licking his lips.

'Yep, as much as you want. There's even nicer hot chocolate at the hotel where I live. This stuff isn't actually that good.' He turned to Eisenstone. 'No offence.'

'It gets better? Impossible.' Phil's miniscule claws tapped on the surface as he scurried to the mug where he clambered up the side and plunged his furry face into its contents, slurping and groaning with pleasure. 'It is so tasty. Hot and chocolatey in equally delightful measure. This is surely the greatest thing in this strange world?'

Eisenstone hadn't moved for quite a while now. A couple of times his mouth closed for a moment as if he was about to speak, but then he just lifted his brow and went back to the same position, chin dangling.

Leaving a trail of soon-to-be-sticky drips, Phil ran back across the desk. He moved on all fours, slightly sideways, slightly forwards, just like a monkey a hundred times his size.

'What else is there?' Phil asked, looking over his shoulder. 'What is the meaning of that box? Where am I? Who are you? I am so very confused. But excited too. Confused and excited. It is about fifty-fifty at present. I must confess, it is quite a pleasant sensation.'

'Stop,' Eisenstone said, finally. 'You can't talk.'

Sharing a look with Tim, who gave a quick shrug, Phil laughed.

'Now, sir, I am just as confused as you are – perhaps more so. But I do appear to be able to talk, quite articulately if I do say so myself.'

'No, you ... can't be real, I'm imagining this.' Eisenstone shook his head. 'Monkey's don't talk. Indeed. And you're a monkey.'

'Finger monkey,' Tim corrected him.

'But, in all seriousness,' Phil said, licking the

last bits of hot chocolate off his paws. 'Who is in charge here?' He pointed quickly between Tim and Eisenstone with one tiny little finger. 'Am I real or am I not?'

'You are,' Tim said, giving him a quick poke. 'Definitely.'

Eisenstone shook his head.

Phil had a long think. 'So, Timothy thinks I am real. I think I am real. I calculate that to be two against one. This is what is called consensus. How do we know anything is real? We just have to come to an agreement.'

'This . . . this is . . . astonishing,' the professor said.

'It's just a tiny little talking monkey,' Tim replied. 'Stranger things have happened.'

'No, Tim,' Eisenstone said. 'No, they haven't.'

Later, when they'd packed everything up and Phil had found a comfortable home in Tim's red-chequered shirt pocket, they left the lab. Outside, beyond a chain-link fence, a black car was parked half on the pavement, half on the road. As Eisenstone slid the imagination box, hidden as always in cardboard, into the boot of his car, Tim caught a glistening glare out of the corner of his eye – a reflection off something. The driver, wearing large sunglasses and a green cap, then lowered an object, started his engine, and drove off out of sight. Tim could have *sworn* he was pointing a camera at them.

'Eisenstone, did you see …' Tim said, frowning, steadily wondering if he was just being paranoid.

'Did I see what?' the professor said, dropping the lid of the boot down with a soft thud. 'What is it?' He seemed worried.

'I just … nothing.'

Tim climbed in and put his seat belt on. Out of fear or perhaps hope, he decided he hadn't seen it. Maybe, like a lot of things that day, his imagination was to blame.

Chapter 6

That evening, people milled around in the Dawn Star's lobby, sipping coffee at tables near the window, reading the paper before dinner and generally doing what hotel guests do – not very much. There was a plan to go back to the lab and Tim could hardly wait ... but first he entered the dining area, walking at a suspiciously slow pace.

Smiling at a waitress, he loitered near the entrance to the kitchen, two swinging doors with little round windows in the top by his side. The coast looked clear. Tim ducked in and crouched behind the main counter. Just above him dishes were being moved and pots were bubbling. On the other side of the silver surface, five or six chefs were busy at work.

Noisily cooking, chatting, pinning orders on the wall and weaving in and out of each other's space.

Tim crawled on all fours across the tiles, to the back end of the kitchen, the walk-in fridge. He had a quick glance over his cover of cardboard boxes to confirm no one was watching, then tugged on the large shiny handle, crawled inside the chilled room and began to search.

Cheesecake, cream, sponge . . . come on . . . where was it?

He stopped. There they were: twenty or so little glass bowls filled with a delicious, literally award-winning dessert – a tiny round sticker on the side of them had the hotel's logo printed on it. The Dawn Star chocolate fudge pudding. Tim grabbed one, wrapped it in some nearby cling film, rammed it in his pocket and swiftly exited the fridge. Head down, he walked briskly towards the swinging doors.

'Hey!' a voice yelled. 'What you doing in my kitchen?'

'I . . .' Tim turned and looked. It was someone he didn't recognise. This must be the new chef Elisa had mentioned, clad in the Dawn Star's whites with a little gold 'DS' sewn into his breast. He was young, perhaps twenty, tall, heavyset, with short black hair and light eyes. '*Your* kitchen?' Tim asked.

The young chef smiled. 'You must be Tim,' he said. 'I'm Stephen Crowfield. Elisa said I might bump into you. She mentioned you've been known to help yourself to certain choice items from the fridge?'

Tim put his hand in his pocket, feeling the cool, expensive glass bowl that housed his freshly stolen loot. 'Well, frankly, that's slander,' he said. 'I wouldn't dream of such a thing.'

Stephen went along with the lie. 'Sure. But maybe I'll make an extra couple of bits and pieces from now on, just in case.'

'Hey, Mr Crowfield, you do what you've got to do to make ends meet.'

'Call me Stephen,' he said.

'Elisa said I should address members of staff formally.'

'Well, I gather you don't always do what she tells you.'

'Stephen,' Tim said, tilting his head, 'you might be right.'

The young chef gave him a quick thumbs-up. 'See you soon, kid.'

Tim turned on his foot and left, thinking that he quite liked Stephen. In comparison he hadn't been fond of the last chef, Antonio, who didn't take too kindly to missing produce.

Back he went through the dining room, the treacherous lava hallway, up the stairs to his bedroom, and kicked the door closed behind him.

'Phil?' Tim whispered. 'Phil, where are you?'

The monkey was sitting on the laptop's keyboard, looking at various pages on the internet. His round eyes had massive white squares in them, reflecting the screen, and his chin dangled in awe.

'Timothy,' Phil said, turning his fuzzy little face, 'I have been on the so-called World Wide Web learning about this universe of yours, as per your instructions. I have seen some good things, and –' he slowly shook his head, and looked down – 'some . . . bad things. And now I have a few enquiries.'

'OK,' Tim replied, sitting on his desk chair in front of the laptop.

Backlit by the computer, Phil swivelled round. Sitting on the keys, not heavy enough to press them, he fitted perfectly on the letters, his feet just resting on the space bar, his bum on G and H.

'Number one,' Phil said, frowning in thought, 'what is the purpose of a bow tie?'

'I . . . um . . . I'm not sure . . . It's a strange question. Maybe they used to hold your shirt on, in the olden days? I don't know if they have a purpose as such – just to look smart I guess.'

'This is in line with what I suspected. I think I quite like them. Next, in a cinema, or a theatre, which armrest belongs to you? Is it the one on the right, or the one on the left?'

'Again,' Tim said, pouting and shrugging, 'I don't really know. I don't think there are written rules.'

'I see. Perhaps there should be, to avoid disputes.' Phil looked down at his feet, wiggling them. 'How many toes does a horse have?'

'None, they have hooves.'

'Goats?'

'Hooves.'

'Bison?'

'Hooves.'

'Ducks?'

'Hoo— No, wait. Three? Or one? I don't know . . . I'm not sure.'

'Where is Funky Town?'

'Phil, right, I can see this going on for a while. Look, I have a present for you,' Tim said.

'Magnificent. Might it be a unicycle, a tiny little unicycle that I could ride around on? Imagine that. The wonder.'

Possible, Tim thought to himself, if he had the imagination box with him. 'Um. No. It's something to eat.'

'As in food?' Phil asked.

'Yes . . . as in food. I remembered how much you liked hot chocolate. So . . .' Tim pulled the pudding from his pocket. 'Ta-da. I got you this. It is probably the greatest chocolatey creation of all time.'

One of Phil's bulbous eyes narrowed – he was intrigued, he rubbed his chin. 'Chocolate you say?'

Tim pulled the cling film off and the monkey

inspected the pudding. He was just about to dip his paw, when there was a loud knock on the door.

'You know the drill,' Tim said, pointing at a small paper cup on his desk. Phil scurried over to it and hid himself underneath. This was their well-rehearsed procedure – Tim knew that Phil, like a lot of recent activities, had to be kept a secret.

He opened the door to see Eisenstone.

'Tim, we must talk,' he said, waving him towards his room.

'Phil, it's OK, you can come out.'

The cup slid across the desk to the edge, where it tilted and then fell: a small shriek came out as it tumbled to the ground. Phil crawled out and brushed himself off, looking slightly embarrassed. Zipping across the carpet, he leapt on to the bed, then on to the cabinet, straight up the spine of the lamp, darting with incredible agility along the frame of a painting and finally landing on Tim's shoulder. He held his shirt pocket open and the creature slid into it. Eisenstone smiled, astonished.

They crossed the hall and sat in room nineteen.

Phil got out and spent some time climbing up and down the curtain.

The professor slouched with a long sigh before he began to talk.

'Tim ... I ... I fear our work might have to be cut short. Things have got a little suspicious. I may have been followed this morning ... I saw a car ...'

'Oh.' Tim instantly changed his mind about the man he'd seen – it wasn't just his imagination. 'I saw a person, outside the lab. I think he was taking photos of us.'

'What?' Eisenstone gasped. 'Why didn't you tell me?'

'I didn't see it clearly. I thought ... I thought maybe I was mistaken.'

'You almost certainly weren't. Listen, this isn't any easy decision, but I'm going to be leaving the country. This hotel, it's not safe any more.'

'Where are you going to go?' Tim felt a sinking feeling in his stomach, selfishly thinking about the imagination box.

'I would be safer – it would be better for the device – if I continued my research in Germany. Yes. I have friends there, fellow physicists. I will

68

be deconstructing the machine. I will remake the prototype over there. Much better.'

Wrapped in both sadness and fear, Tim sighed.

'I will be back, and I will indeed of course be in contact. Remember, you're the only person who has been able to make this thing work. You and my invention, well, indeed, you belong together.'

'Will I be all right?' Tim asked. 'Do these people know about me?'

Eisenstone gradually shook his head, faster and faster. 'No, no,' he said. 'Even if they've seen us together, there would be no reason to suspect you were behind any success. I know this is hard, but what I'm really trying to say is—'

'What do clouds actually want?' Phil asked. Tim turned to see the monkey looking pensively out of the window.

'Tim,' Eisenstone whispered, drawing his attention back, 'listen, you *must* keep Phil secret. You hear me? It's crucial. Crucial indeed. I don't want to scare you, but you really can't trust anyone. I mean that. Remember it. Don't trust *anyone*.'

'I understand,' Tim said.

'We'll do our final tests tomorrow morning. This is a minor setback in a grand journey, Tim, you understand? This machine isn't merely a bottomless toy box. When it's refined, when it's properly understood, it is going to be a revolution. Imagine, one in every home – what that would mean for those in need … commerce, industry, medicine, entertainment. There's no part of society this gadget won't affect.'

Tim hadn't considered it before, but the professor was right. The box wasn't just a toy. It was so much more than that.

'We'll get there,' Eisenstone added. 'Whatever it takes. But you've got to keep what we've been doing quiet – I know it'll be tempting to tell all your friends, but you mustn't.'

'All my friends already know,' he replied.

There was a few seconds of silence and the professor smiled strangely – as though he was both happy and sad simultaneously.

*

That night, in bed, Tim stared for hours at a small slither of paint in the corner of his ceiling. When, finally, he fell asleep, he returned to a nightmare he'd had countless times when he was small. He was always in his most recent home, completely alone, walking up stairs. But it never ended; the steps just went on and on and on. And then, at some point, he'd hear a sound – something behind, chasing him up the infinite staircase.

The dream always ended the same way – the shadowy, formless beast would gain on him, the ground would become thick, like running through treacle, he'd turn to face it and he'd wake just before the creature pounced.

Gasping, lifting his head from his pillow, he realised he was safe in his room. It was what Eisenstone had said, he told himself, about being followed, about being in danger – that's why he'd had the nightmare again. For the first time in a long time, Tim was scared.

Chapter 7

In their final morning of testing at the lab, Tim created a number of items. He struggled a little with a few of them, but once he properly focused, he was eventually able to make everything asked of him. And each time, Eisenstone seemed more impressed than the last.

'Amazing. Incredible. Extraordinary,' he'd say, as he flicked open the lid.

Phil too, was taken aback by what he was seeing. All the creations – some hydrogen, a piece of coal and water – were a perfect success, except one. Tim was asked to make an iron nail. As he was imagining it, he heard a seagull squawk outside the window and before he knew it he was thinking about the beach.

When they opened the lid there was a lump of what could be, and indeed was, described as 'disgusting gloop'. It looked like green honey, but it had little patches of sand and tiny plants a bit like seaweed. Also it smelled like vinegar and candyfloss. Most unpleasant. This mishmash of thoughts was a stark example of how important it was for him to stay focused on the object he wished to create.

Just before lunchtime, Eisenstone lowered sheets of notes and various documents into a shredder, making a curly mass of white paper. He deleted all his records from the computer, and pulled stacks of CDs and tapes off his shelf, ramming them into his case.

After his frantic packing ahead of his flight to Germany the following afternoon, he turned to the desk where the imagination box stood proudly in the centre, the reader, wrapped in its wire, placed on top. The final item.

'It's going to be sad to say goodbye,' the professor said.

'I know.' Tim wasn't sure if he was talking to the box, or to him, or to both.

'Right, indeed, all right, wait here, I'll be five minutes, I need to get some tools to . . . dismantle it,' he sighed.

Eisenstone left the room, leaving Tim and Phil by themselves. For a few seconds they both stared at the machine in silence, Tim listening only to his thoughts and the ticking of the clock.

'So,' the monkey said, pacing along the desk, 'why not make something? Might be your last chance?'

'Yes,' Tim said, standing, placing the reader on his head. 'Great minds think alike.'

'Might I submit chocolate as a possible choice?'

'No, I'm not going to make chocolate – we can get chocolate at home.'

'Just a bit, just make a *little bit* of chocolate.'

'Phil, if I was going to make chocolate I'd make a lot. But it'd be a wasted opportunity.'

'Fine,' he huffed.

'I think . . . I think I know what to create,' Tim said.

Stepping forwards, eyes shut, he took a long breath in. His hand hovered above the round green button.

Nodding to himself a final time, he knew exactly what he wanted. It was the only logical thing he could make. And, if he was honest with himself, he was actually surprised he hadn't thought of doing it before. It seemed so obvious. Bending the end of his index finger back, whitening his knuckle, he pressed the button with firm certainty.

The beep followed by the cacophony of sound and commotion as it burst into life was now completely familiar to Tim. Stepping back, he shared a smile with Phil. The machine rumbled and jigged around, constructing his final thought.

'What did you go for?' the monkey asked.

'You'll see.' Tim took the complicated, multi-panelled reader off his head and placed it on the table.

They both watched as the device fizzled to a stop and the blinking light returned.

It was done.

When Tim opened the lid, the first thing that greeted his eyes was a large black question mark, printed on the side of his creation, which filled the box. Joy danced through Tim's entire being as a drumroll thumped eagerly in his head. It had worked.

'I've done what the genie forbids,' Tim whispered.

'Ah, of course you have,' Phil said. 'Forgive me, but what does the genie forbid?'

'I've wished . . . for more wishes,' Tim said, lifting the cube out. 'I have created my very own imagination box.'

'Well, I say, that is terrifically clever, Timothy. Top drawer.'

Tim held up a slightly smaller, curvier version of the original. It looked neater and all together more finished, packaged in sleek silver metal – modern and simple.

Tim reached out and ran his hand across the smooth surface. He found the switch for the hatch right where he had imagined it would be. It only took the lightest of touches and the top slid back in a far cooler way than the original model's lid. It was like a futuristic automatic door, silently opening and folding neatly away. A complicated mechanism, the workings of which Tim did not even consciously understand, must be hidden somewhere in the walls of the box.

From inside Tim carefully pulled out a normal-looking black beanie hat. The letters 'TIB' were written across the front in tiny white print.

'Wireless,' he muttered to himself, realising he could remotely use the box and no one would know he was doing so. He turned the hat over in his hands, stretching the material a little, examining it.

Brushing his hair flat, he slowly lowered the beanie on to his head then put the new imagination box in an old rucksack they found in one of the cupboards. He smiled at himself in the mirror, with his black hat, his red-chequered shirt and his new favourite gadget slung over his back. With a nod, he tightened the straps.

'Looking good, sir,' Phil said.

The professor's footsteps approached the lab, so Tim whipped the hat from his head and stuffed it in his back pocket, feeling guilty.

When Eisenstone returned, he quickly got to work unscrewing the bolts and unplugging all the components from his prototype. He was so preoccupied with packing he didn't even notice that Tim had the rucksack hanging from his shoulders.

He was almost certain that the professor wouldn't want him to have his own imagination box, but Tim couldn't just let go of the greatest toy in the world. Besides, he could keep a secret and, really, who would suspect a ten-year-old boy of possessing such a thing?

'Time to go.' Eisenstone held the door open as Tim gathered up the remainder of his things. He paused for one last look at the room, all lit up, full of so many different contraptions and components – the accumulation of so much work.

'Ready,' he said, turning his back on the lab.

The lights snapped off and the door slowly hissed shut with a final clunk that quietly echoed down the hallway.

'Here,' the professor said when they were back at the Dawn Star, in the corridor between their rooms. 'This is where I'm going to be working, in Germany.' He gave Tim a business card, which he slid into his shirt pocket. 'My flight is tomorrow afternoon. I'll see you in the morning. We'll say goodbye properly then.'

After he'd said goodnight, Tim pretty much dived into his bedroom. He'd been shaking with anticipation in the car on the way back to the hotel, desperate to try what he'd made. He removed his imagination box from the bag and placed it right in the centre of his bedside cabinet, paying careful attention to its positioning. The hat felt snug on his head and, as he took a step away, Phil keenly watched from the bed.

'Ready?'

'Let us proceed,' the monkey replied. 'In the interest of discretion, I suggest we keep quiet.'

'OK,' Tim said, wiggling the fabric reader a little.

He closed his eyes and tilted his head, imagining deeply.

The machine hummed and he marvelled at how much quicker and quieter it was compared with the prototype. The lid slid open and Tim pulled out a brand-new set of pencils, ten shades of every colour of the rainbow.

He made all sorts of stuff: silly sunglasses; cool

sunglasses; a shoe; a tiny little chair for Phil; for some reason, nail polish; a few bags of candyfloss; a treasure map ('we must remember to follow that,' Tim said, throwing it down on the pile); a packet of cheese and *vinegar* crisps; a tiny little bed for Phil; a pocket book all about lesser-known camel facts ('Asian camels have two humps, and Arabian camels have just one,' Tim read); a tiny little unicycle for Phil; some glow-in-the-dark ants; a tomato-flavoured strawberry; vice versa; a six-and-a-half pound note; the other shoe—

Tim stopped and stroked his chin, dropping the final item on the ground behind him.

'What's on your mind?' Phil asked.

'Well, all this stuff is great and all, but I can't help thinking . . .'

'Oh yes, thinking is essential.'

'No, I mean, I just wonder what it *can't* make.'

Tim remembered some of Eisenstone's examples as he closed his eyes and tested the limits. This time the imagination box seemed to strain. It rumbled along the cabinet, wiggling side to side, constructing his thought. After a few seconds, he stepped forwards and opened the lid.

'Ha.'

'What is it?' Phil asked.

'Water.' Tim frowned, tilting the box and swirling the liquid. 'I tried to make hot ice. And I got ... water.'

'Well, to me that makes perfect sense.'

But somehow Tim felt he had failed. This wasn't what he'd pictured. 'Yeah, but I imagined ice in the shape of fire. It was so clear. So vivid.'

'Maybe it melted?'

It was a strange feeling having the box 'disobey' him – it was as though he had been overruled by a higher authority. Reality can be a real spoilsport. He thought of the accidental seaside sludge and wondered what other mistakes it might conjure up, what other ways it could shine a light on to the imperfections of his mind.

After his frenzy of creation, Tim hid as much as he could fit in his wardrobe. Then he put the box under his bed, before collapsing on top, fully clothed and still wearing his reader hat. It had been fun, but he still felt an emptiness about Eisenstone leaving (made worse by the fact he had done all *this* behind his back). He knew that at some point everyone leaves, but he never expected the professor's departure from his life to affect him quite as much as it did. It was silly, really – he'd only known him for a matter of days – and yet. His eyes fixed once again on a flake of paint peeling in the corner of his ceiling. The sound of the hotel's pipes digesting under his floorboards was usually comforting, but not tonight.

Troubled, but snug in his new reader hat, Tim drifted away from reality and into a dark place. His nightmare started as it always did – he was home alone, now in the Dawn Star, at the foot of the infinite staircase . . . and *something* was hot on his heels.

It was early in the morning and he woke with a gasp. His head was hot, sweaty, from the beanie – he pulled it off, dropping it on his bedside cabinet. The memory of his dream made him shudder as he swung his legs out and stood up. It felt somehow more real than the last one. Stepping out of his bedroom to head for breakfast, he felt another wave of doubt about creating his own imagination box in secret. Perhaps it would be better to tell the professor, perhaps he'd—

Tim stopped in the hallway. Room nineteen's door was wide open and, inside, the hotel's head chambermaid Mary was changing the bedding.

'Where is ... where's Eisenstone?' Tim thought aloud, peering around.

Mary frowned then lifted up the corner of the sheet, to look under. This was clearly meant to be funny, but Tim didn't even twitch a smile. 'He's gone,' she said. 'Haven't seen him. He left hours ago.' She finished routinely tucking everything in too tight, then pushed her trolley past him.

The professor had gone without saying goodbye – how could he do that? No. Something wasn't right. Eisenstone wouldn't just leave, not like that, he wouldn't ...

But, right then, his thoughts were interrupted by an almighty screech from somewhere in the building. A woman screaming, again and again, louder and louder.

Chapter 8

Through room nineteen's window, Tim saw a flurry
of feathers fall from the Dawn Star Hotel's gutters as
pigeons erupted into the sky, startled by the screaming
inside. Another loud, blood-curdling yell made it
easy to follow. Without thinking, Tim overtook the
chambermaid and headed for the stairs. The terrible
noise was coming from the ground floor.

Tim arrived to find Elisa and Donald, the new
consultant, already there. Mary was looking on from
the end of the hall, concerned, but keeping a distance.
The new chef, Stephen, peered through the lobby's
oak doors and guests were beginning to open their
rooms.

'What's going on?' Tim asked.

'We're not sure. Go back upstairs,' Elisa said. She banged on the wood. 'Is everything all right in there?'

The door swung open – a woman ran into the hallway, clutching her hair.

'Are you all right?' Elisa asked. 'What's wrong?'

'There's an animal in there. A monster! A thing. I don't know what it is!' Her fear had now turned to anger. 'It's gone back in the vents. I want you to know that I am suing!'

Elisa and Donald entered room four. Tim went in behind them, looking straight to the vent near the floor. The metal grid that opened up to the hotel's ventilation system was damaged – the slats had been bent, snapped, twisted open and a large hole made in the centre. It would have taken a lot of force.

Tim turned, thinking, fearing, realising. He felt dizzy, sick. Was this still a nightmare? He clenched his teeth. Wake up, wake up, he thought.

He ran straight back upstairs. Rushing, he didn't even see Mary's trolley parked outside his room and collided with it, sending all her cleaning bottles, cloths and collected towels across the carpet. Too panicked to pick it all up, he burst into his room and slammed the door behind him.

Instantly, he swooped to the corner where, near the skirting board, the brass slats of the ventilation grill were broken – just like the ones in room four.

'Timothy,' Phil said from the bedside cabinet, 'what is happening?'

Tim scanned the floor, the walls, even the ceiling. His hands were shaking as he knelt down, pushing his shoulder under his bed frame to pull out the rucksack that housed his imagination box. His fingers passed over the frayed threads. It had been torn, ripped open – the zip still intact.

'Oh no,' he said to himself. 'It's . . . it's real.'

'What is?' Phil asked.

Tim didn't answer, he just grabbed a stack of books and rammed them against the vent. Then he got a chair and wedged it between the barricade and his chest of drawers.

'Has something got into your room?'

'Worse,' Tim said. 'Something's got *out*. I . . . I fell asleep with the reader on, my reader hat,' he explained.

'I think . . . I think I might have accidently created my own worst nightmare.'

'Well fiddle my sticks,' Phil exclaimed. 'This sounds far from ideal.'

Tim's heart was thudding in his chest. Each beat was like being punched – he felt it in his mouth. 'I used to have this nightmare, when I was little,' he said, staring at the wall. 'I was home, alone, and I was running up the stairs. I was being chased by something. By a . . . a monster.'

The monkey, who'd clambered on to the bed, glanced over his shoulder, unsettled by Tim's distress.

'It's like . . . I always wake up before it gets me.' Tim tried to picture it in his mind. The image was unclear. He couldn't put his finger on exactly what it looked like, or what made it so terrifying. 'It's never . . . it's made of shadows. It's a blur.'

He couldn't really describe in words what it was. It was more of a feeling . . . of dread, hopelessness, loneliness.

'Basically,' Tim sighed, 'it's not a good thing. Maybe Eisenstone was right. Maybe this is what he meant about the possible dangers, what it could do in the wrong hands?'

'Right,' Phil replied. 'And this thing, it is loose in the hotel?'

'Yes,' Tim said. 'It is loose in the hotel.'

Sitting against the wall, with his knees pulled to his chest, Tim managed to calm himself. A minute or so later, outside his door, Mary shouted what he assumed was a Spanish swear word. She'd obviously just discovered he'd knocked over her trolley when he'd rushed back to his room. He pushed himself to his feet.

'Mary,' Tim said, stepping into the hall, 'I'm sorry. I didn't see it.'

'It's OK,' she replied. 'These things, they happen.'

She was on her hands and knees, retrieving everything. Feeling responsible, Tim was about to help her. But, on the carpet, among all the bleach bottles and cleaning cloths, he spotted something. Something that somehow made him completely forget about the monster he'd accidently created. The minute hand froze. Time stopped. Staring, fixated on the item that Mary had obviously found in room nineteen, Tim's shallow breaths stuttered.

Swallowing, he reached down and placed his hand on top of the silver watch. He slowly lifted and turned it to look on the underside.

The letters 'P' and 'E' were carved on the back, engraved in a delicate font.

Chapter 9

Tim wasn't at all surprised when Eisenstone's mobile went straight to voicemail. He dropped his bedroom phone down with a clunk and sat, illuminated by his lamp, staring down at the old pocket watch.

'Timothy,' Phil said, running up his trousers, his lap and then on to his desk. He sat on top of the watch, oblivious to its importance. 'That thing, that yellow thing, the nabina, banboba, branoony?'

'Banana.'

'Yes, that, the banana, it was most lovely. It felt right, eating it, if you can comprehend such a notion . . . it just felt somehow right.'

The banana Tim had left for Phil on the desk was covered in tiny bite holes; he'd clearly enjoyed it.

'You are a monkey. That's what you eat.'

'Well, it was delightful, and I thank you for it.'

Tim's gaze rested on nowhere. 'Peter Eisenstone . . . it was his father's watch,' he said, thinking aloud.

'Yes, an excellent observation, Timothy, well done,' Phil replied, clearly still daydreaming about bananas. 'Wait, what?'

'The watch. It belonged to Eisenstone's father.'

'Which watch? Hehe, that is a pleasure to pronounce. Which watch?'

'His watch. His silver pocket watch.'

'I am terribly afraid I am not familiar with it.'

'Phil, you're sitting on it.'

He cocked his head, looking down at his seat. 'Ah, yes. Of course. Eisenstone's watch. I conclude that he left it here.'

'Yeah. And still no sign of him.'

'OK . . . is this a problem? I appear to be missing something.' The banana caught Phil's eye. He scuttled across the desk, his claws tapping on the wood all the way to the fruit. He began tugging handfuls out and shovelling them in his mouth. 'People do change their plans, it's not unheard of. Oh whiskers on biscuits,' he exclaimed, 'this is just so delicious!'

'Eisenstone specifically said he never, ever goes anywhere without it. I know I have an overactive imagination. I *know* that. But . . . but something still doesn't feel right. He wouldn't leave without saying goodbye and he certainly wouldn't leave his watch.'

Phil turned his head further round than a person could, his mouth covered in glistening food. 'So, something has gone wrong? Or maybe he just forgot it. It is a mystery. Who knows? Timothy, how about I sit here and politely wait while you go and get me some cake.'

'What? No.'

'I see. A reasonable response. So, about this watch, what is the situation?'

'He said he may have been in danger. And he said that he would never be apart from his watch. But he clearly is. That's all we know for sure. So he goes to Germany because he was scared – what if he doesn't get there? His mobile is off, and there's no other way to get through to him.'

'I suggest you simply wait for his call,' Phil shrugged.

'That's not good advice. I can't sit here doing nothing.'

'If you knew where he was meant to be, you could just ring and ask if he is there, then ask about the watch. That, my good friend, would be problem solved.'

'But that's the whole thing, I don't know—' Tim stopped. 'The card. He gave me a business card with the lab's name on it. The German lab.'

He shoved his swivel chair back and went straight to his wardrobe, sliding his shirts left then right, looking for the one he was wearing when Eisenstone left.

'It's not here,' Tim sighed. 'I might have put it in the laundry basket . . .'

'Why do you not simply *imagine* a new card into existence?'

'I did look at it, so perhaps the details are in my brain somewhere . . .'

It worked: Tim successfully recreated the business

card and, later that day – around the time the professor should've arrived in Germany – he punched in the number on his phone. A chirpy man answered.

'*Guten Tag*, Webster-Jones Inc.'

'Um. Yes. Hello. I am looking to speak with Eisenstone, Professor George Eisenstone. He's my . . . grandfather.' Tim shrugged at Phil. 'Have I got the right number?'

'Hang on, I'll put you through.'

There was a long dialling tone, followed by a clunk, and then someone else picked up the line.

'Hello!'

'Hello, yes, may I speak to George Eisenstone. Professor. He's English. He's working there. I'm his . . . grandson.' He figured it would make more sense if they thought he was family, instead of a neurotic child with an overdeveloped imagination.

'Ah, I am afraid not. You're right. He was *meant* to be here. In fact, he and I were meant to be working together this month. I *just* this moment returned from the airport. He didn't arrive.'

'You haven't heard from him at all?'

94

'Not a peep – he called me out of the blue earlier in the week, saying he needed to get away. Perhaps he changed his mind. Perhaps he decided to stay with his family there? His daughter lives quite close to him, as you know – she's your mother, yes?'

'What?' Tim asked.

'Sarah Eisenstone?'

'Who?'

'Your mother. George's daughter ... you said he was your grandfather?'

Tim's eyes widened.

'No. Yes. I am. Yes. My mother. His daughter. It makes sense doesn't it? What with me being his grandson. That's how families work ...'

'To be honest I thought he only had one granddaughter, but you're clearly a boy.'

He quickly considered putting on a high voice and pretending to be a girl, but decided it was probably better to continue down his original path of lies.

'Nope,' Tim said. 'Granddad only has me. No granddaughters at all.'

'Must have misheard. Well I can tell you, I saw

everyone else get off that flight, and he was not on it. I am sure he has his reasons. It is possible he's had some kind of brainwave and has locked himself away at his home to work on something incredible. He has done this in the past. The man is a workaholic. When you see him, tell him Benjamin is not so happy.'

'Will do.'

'Goodbye, young man.'

The phone stayed against Tim's ear, the dialling tone hummed for a few seconds and then cut to silence.

Perhaps the professor didn't escape soon enough, Tim thought, or perhaps there *was* an innocent explanation. Maybe Benjamin was right – maybe Eisenstone had simply retreated to his home to work. But . . . the watch.

'He never made it to Germany.'

'Then,' Phil said, 'let us find him.'

Tim paced across the hotel lobby, waiting for his moment. He had concluded that, in light of Benjamin's comments, the best place to start, as with most possible missing person's cases, was at his home.

When the young receptionist left her post and walked into the office behind to do some photocopying, Tim sat on the counter and swung his legs over. He went straight to the computer, checking over his shoulder to make sure she wasn't looking. Clicking the 'Guest logs' icon, he was presented with a huge spreadsheet. A quick search, typing 'Eise', and the professor's details zipped to the top. After jotting down the address, he closed the file, stood and rolled over the wooden counter again, landing smoothly just as the receptionist returned. She smiled at him, completely oblivious.

As he passed back through the lobby, he spotted Donald Pinkman, dressed smartly, sitting on one of the tables, filling out some paperwork. The consultant had a large bald spot and a slender frame – his thin legs were crossed, almost wrapped entirely around one another.

'Ah, Tim,' he said, waving him over with a smile. 'Come and sit down – have some tea.'

Reluctantly, Tim stepped to the table and sat. He would rather carry on with his investigation, but Donald seemed insistent.

'I wanted to talk to you about the Dawn Star,' he said, pouring the tea, the pot's china lid clinking as he set it down. 'As you know, as consultant, it is my job to make things run a little smoother here. Terrible business with the incident in room four. I shudder to think what kind of vermin could be on the loose. Anyway, I understand sometimes you like to explore – go places you ought not.' His tone was like that of a teacher, speaking down to Tim. Speaking sternly. Almost rudely, Tim thought.

'Well,' he replied. 'This *is* my home.'

'Of course,' Donald said, his voice overly gentle, patronising. He smiled just with his mouth, his eyes remaining still. 'I understand that. But you must appreciate that this is a functioning business. It isn't professional to have a child running around. *Stealing*.'

Right then, Tim decided he didn't like Donald. What Tim did or didn't do at the hotel was between him and Elisa, he thought.

'Yeah,' Tim said. 'I'll keep that in mind.'

'Oh, I wouldn't want you to take it to heart, you must not feel . . . a prisoner in your own home. I just think it would pay for you to *keep your nose out of other people's business.*' Donald maintained eye contact, almost daring Tim to say something defiant. But, despite the significant temptation, he remained polite.

'You're right,' Tim said. 'I will do my best not to interfere with the running of the hotel.'

There was a long pause – Donald narrowed his eyes, as if waiting for a punchline. 'Good,' he finally said, assuming his warning had worked. 'Anyway, enough about that. Your mother told me you're a keen artist.'

'That's highly unlikely,' Tim replied.

'Oh really, why's that?' Donald asked, slurping his tea. All his limbs seemed a little too long, his large foot swinging as he spoke.

'Elisa isn't my mother,' he replied.

'She isn't?'

'No, I'm adopted. Anyway, I've got—'

'I also wanted to talk to you about Professor Eisenstone.'

'Really, why?' Tim snapped, then coughed and calmed a little, realising he might have sounded too eager. 'Why?'

'Oh . . . no real reason.' Donald ran his long finger around the rim of his mug. 'The man fascinates me. Elisa tells me you've helped him with his latest work. Judging by his field – nanotechnology, quantum physics – it must have been an amazing opportunity. What did you get to do?'

The lie Eisenstone had suggested came to him quickly, like a reflex. 'He's been doing a study on children. It's a reading study. I had to read. He's researching how children learn.'

'Really? That sounds exciting.' Donald's eyes – so brown they were black – grew.

'Nah. There was nothing exciting about all that work. It was dull, if anything. Dull and boring,' Tim said. The professor's words echoed in his head: this had to be a secret, just for now.

Donald squinted and Tim got a strange feeling that he was scrutinising him a little too closely, analysing every aspect of his face – looking for the lie he'd just told. It must just be his guilty conscience though, Tim told himself. There was no reason for Donald to suspect anything. Nervously Tim shuffled in his seat – the prolonged staring made him feel uneasy.

'Anyway. Enjoy the tea.' Tim stood, and picked up one of the chocolate biscuits from the table.

'Remember what I said. I've got my eye on you, Mr Hart.'

'Um . . .' Tim replied, thinking it a strange thing to say. 'Thank you.'

He didn't turn back but felt that unbroken gaze following him all the way to the broad oak doors that led to the lava hallway. What a weirdo, Tim thought, arriving at his bedroom.

'Phil?' he whispered, stepping inside. 'Where are you?'

A low groan came from his desk as a paper cup and a couple of pencils rolled across the wood, revealing Phil, curled up. Another long moaning sound arose from the tiny monkey, clutching his golf-ball sized belly.

'Oh, Timothy, help me . . . I am in jolly big trouble.'

'What's wrong?' Tim ran to his desk, terrified, flicking on his lamp.

Leaning just his head, unable to move, Phil pointed at an empty glass bowl that had once contained a Dawn Star chocolate fudge pudding. Now it just had brown marks with tiny tracks where he'd clawed out every last bit of cake. With Stephen Crowfield in the kitchen – someone nice enough to turn a blind eye – there had been a steady supply.

'Where's it gone?' Tim asked, lifting the bowl and searching behind his mug full of pens. Phil just shook his head and looked down at himself.

'No,' Tim said. 'Impossible.'

'I thought that too, Timothy. I thought there is no way that amount of cake could possibly fit in such a tiny little monkey. But, alas, it has happened. It is now past tense. It has been committed to reality – there is no room for speculation. All that cake *can* fit in a tiny little monkey. But at what cost Timothy? *At what cost?*'

'You're just full up. You'll be fine. Now, I think we should—'

'No, Tim, *no*, you do not understand ... so much ... so much cake. It is quite a big portion for a human, but for me?'

'I brought you a chocolate biscuit from downstairs but I suppose you don't want it now,' Tim said.

'Well, come along, slow down a minute, Timothy,' Phil pulled himself to his feet, like a fat, drunk cowboy. 'I never said I didn't want any. I need fuel for our investigation.'

'True. I managed to find Eisenstone's address.'

'Well, as they say, it is seldom dandy to dawdle,' the monkey said, approaching the biscuit. 'Let us venture onwards.'

Chapter 10

The bus stopped with a hiss in front of a picturesque house with white-painted bricks and a neat picket fence. A gentle breeze rocked an apple tree in a nearby garden slowly from side to side, leaves rustling. Tim, dressed in his red-chequered shirt, wearing his reader hat and carrying his imagination box in his backpack, looked up and down the quiet street and then set off walking, counting the numbers on the houses. Six, eight, ten, twelve.

Tim still felt a little guilty about the bus ticket – he had been short of cash but luckily he 'remembered' he had a pound in his bag. This was, no matter how you measured it, a crime. You are simply not allowed to pay for things with fake money – that's an actual proper law. Even though it was indistinguishable from a real one, it was still counterfeit. Tim's only comfort was that, even if he confessed, no one would believe he'd imagined the coin into existence.

This wasn't his only breach of the rules that day as, instead of trying to explain the situation to Elisa, he'd told her he was nipping briefly to the shop at the end of the street. Far simpler this way, he concluded.

After a short walk, he arrived at number eighteen – Eisenstone's house. There was no answer when he rang the doorbell, as he'd feared. Benjamin had suggested on the phone that the professor might have returned home, to his office, to work on something. Tim, knowing what he knew, found that to be quite unlikely. Still, he followed the lead as he had to be sure – he had to see for himself ... or, rather, his monkey had to.

'Phil, you're up,' he said to his pocket, glancing quickly over his shoulder.

'Right you are,' the monkey replied, poking his head out, blinking in the afternoon sun.

'Remember, find his office. You're looking for

anything out of the ordinary. Has Eisenstone returned home at any point? Any clues at all.'

The monkey leapt from Tim's pocket and on to his hand. He held him up to the letter box, lifting the shiny bronze flap as he had another quick look around. Carefully, Phil crawled through the slot, the horizontal metal door snapping shut behind him.

He was inside.

Tim stepped round to the living-room window, where he cupped his face and watched the monkey clamber off a mountain of mail, then scurry into the living room – he looked tiny, a mere shadow darting across the carpet.

'Hello?' a small voice said, from behind. 'Who are you?'

Spinning, Tim saw a girl around his age. After a moment he recognised her from the photo he'd seen in the lab – it was Eisenstone's granddaughter. She had tightly curled blonde hair, kept back by a thick purple hairband. Her baggy, blue-and-white polka-dot dress and her hairstyle reminded Tim of someone from the past. A 1940s swing dancer or something similar.

'Oh. Sorry,' Tim said, startled. 'My name is Timothy Hart. I'm … I'm looking for George Eisenstone.'

'He's not here,' Dee said. 'He's away.'

'Do you know where he's gone?' Tim asked, testing the water.

'To Germany, on business.' Wrong. 'Think he'll be back in a few weeks.'

For a brief moment Tim felt the urge to tell her the truth, but knew that'd invariably open up a big can of questions – the answers to which were explicitly secret.

'You're his granddaughter?' Tim said.

'Yes. Dee. How do you know him?'

'It's … a long story.'

'Well, I'll let him know you stopped by. Anyway, good to meet you.' She tilted her head awkwardly, clearly wanting to get past, to the door. 'I've got to feed Jingles now … so …'

Tim frowned. 'Sorry, what? Who's Jingles?'

'Jingles? She's granddad's cat.'

'What … what do you mean?' Tim shook his head.

'Um.' Dee seemed confused by the concern. 'I don't know if there's a simpler way of saying it . . . he possesses a feline? Like a dog, but smaller and . . . like . . . a cat.'

'Oh no.'

'Not a fan?' Dee said, pushing the key into the lock and swinging the door open.

Tim then, without thinking, pushed his way into the house behind her, desperate to make sure Phil was still in one piece.

'Um,' she said, stumbling aside. 'What are you doing?'

'I . . .' He realised how dodgy he must have looked, barging into the building like that.

Then his eyes locked on Phil, loitering about in the kitchen doorway. Phew. The monkey tried to appear inconspicuous, staring up at the ceiling and whistling.

Behind him, however, suspended in the shadow of the counter, was a pair of glistening green eyes. Slowly the cat flowed out, moving like water, with predatory ease.

'Phil, run!' Tim shouted.

As Dee turned, Jingles was airborne, flying across the kitchen. Phil was bashed across the tiles by swinging claws, spinning on his back. Jumping up to his feet, he ran.

'Was that a mouse?' Dee yelled, stepping quickly further inside.

The monkey barrelled into the living room, zig-zagging. In a blink the cat darted after him, missing once again, rolling and bashing into the coffee table, things slipping and bouncing off. Dodging the TV remote, Phil zipped across the hallway and leapt towards the stairs, diving through the wooden uprights of the banister.

Jingles, on the other hand, wasn't quite small enough to fit, but followed regardless. After a very ungraceful thud, the cat spiralled to the ground, dazed, before bolting back into the kitchen, seemingly defeated – perhaps even embarrassed.

The whole thing lasted no more than a few seconds. And, although he was sure she'd probably seen Phil clearly, Tim still jumped between Dee and the stairs, blocking her view.

'What was that?'

'What was what?'

'That animal on the stairs,' she said, plainly. 'The one right behind you. You're standing in the way of it. If you just step aside, we can see it.'

'Oh,' Tim said. '*That*. Well. That's my, um, pet mouse. Yep. Little Phil.'

She nodded, frowning. 'It didn't look like a mouse. And you're quite clearly lying.'

Tim coughed awkwardly. 'I'm . . . not . . . lying.'

'You just did it again,' she said, pointing. 'Your eyes. You looked up and right when you were talking. You see, up and left means you're accessing a memory, up and right means you're accessing the creative part of your brain, i.e. lying. Body language. It's incredibly important.'

There was a long drawn-out pause while they simply stared at each other. Tim closed his eyes, defeated but strangely pleased to share his secret with Dee. 'Right,' he said. 'I did lie. It's not a mouse, but it's complicated, I can't—'

'No, wait,' Dee said to herself. 'Hang on. It's the

other way around. Up and right is memory, up and *left* is lying. So, I would have said you were being honest. But, then you just said you *were* lying . . . Soooo. Let's take a little walk down, down, down –' she did a strange dance with each word – 'to truth town.'

Eisenstone had told him he couldn't trust *anyone*, but surely telling Dee, his own granddaughter, wouldn't cause too much trouble. 'What's your favourite animal?' Tim asked.

She bobbed her head in thought. 'I don't know, um, foxes . . . or . . . are we allowed mythical creatures? Then it's Pegasus probably. Pegasus. What's the plural? Pegasi? Pegasuses? Pegapods? I suppose there can't be a plural, as there was only one. Anyway, them. Horses with wings. Although, I suppose, foxes are quite cool. But . . . no wings . . . Oh. I don't know. I'd need to do a pros and cons list to give a definitive answer. What's *your* favourite animal?'

Tim stepped to the side, exposing Phil standing at their level on the stairs. 'Finger monkeys.'

'That is amazing.' Dee leant in close, astonished. 'What's its name?'

'Phil,' Tim said.

'Wow. Where . . . where did you get it?'

'Oh, I am fine by the way, guys,' Phil yelled. 'I haven't just narrowly avoided getting devoured or anything.'

Dee's mouth sprang wide open. She rubbed her eyes, blinking. 'Right,' she said, closing the front door and turning to them. 'Tell me *exactly* what's going on.'

Chapter 11

Once Dee had heard Phil speak, there was no point in trying to lie. So, in the professor's kitchen, Tim explained everything to her. The box, the sausage, the nightmare, Eisenstone's disappearance – everything. And it felt good. It felt like he'd unlocked a knot in his stomach.

'Look,' she sighed after he'd finished. 'I don't know if you've got something wrong with you ... or what. I don't know what this is, or how you've managed to make that creature speak, but—'

'You don't believe me?'

'My granddad invented a box that creates whatever you imagine?' she laughed. 'Of course I don't believe you.'

After a while, however, she gave Tim the benefit of the doubt and allowed him to have a look upstairs in Eisenstone's house. They discovered that his office had been trashed – someone had come in through the window and messily searched the place.

Dee then suggested, perhaps quite rightly Tim thought, that they call the police. He remembered the officer who'd come to the lab to discuss the stolen briefcase with the professor. 'We should call Inspector Kane,' he concluded.

Tim returned to the hotel and later Dee and her mother, Eisenstone's daughter Sarah, arrived. Inspector Kane came shortly after, wearing his long coat and with his badge on his belt.

The policeman briefly questioned Elisa and then Sarah, Dee, Kane and Tim then went to the function room, the very place he met Eisenstone, where it would be quiet. They sat around a small table near the stage, and all had a good look at the professor's watch. Stephen Crowfield brought a tray of tea and biscuits from the kitchen, but only Kane had any. He seemed the only one who wasn't too worried to eat – this was the kind of case he handled every day, Tim thought.

'Now, Tim,' Kane said, opening his notepad and clicking his pen. 'When did you last see George Eisenstone?'

'It was last night.'

'I see. And the work you were doing with him? You were helping him at his lab, is that correct?'

Tim's heart thumped. He had a moment of eye contact with Dee. He didn't know whether he should lie or tell the truth.

'Yes, we were . . . we were . . .'

Sarah interrupted. 'My father was working on a learning paper,' she said. 'It was a study on children, how they read, how they learn.'

Tim saw in her eyes that this wasn't a lie. This is what Sarah believed. Eisenstone hadn't even told his *own daughter* about his work. That's how secret it was, he thought, feeling a wave of pride, like hot tea going down, followed quickly by rumbling panic.

'Yes,' Tim said, his hand trembling under the table. 'It was just a study on learning.'

The lie tasted terrible. He swallowed hard. Eisenstone's warnings about secrecy rattled in his brain once again.

The interview lasted about twenty more minutes. Inspector Kane spoke for a while about his investigation, what he'd be doing over the coming days before Eisenstone was declared 'officially' missing.

'There's quite a procedure to go through,' he explained, 'and nearly always there's a reasonable explanation.'

This offered no comfort.

People do just disappear, Tim thought – he knew that well. After all, that's what happened with his father. There can be no 'reasonable' explanation, nor any explanation at all. People just go.

Before they left, Inspector Kane, Sarah, Elisa and Donald talked by the front door in the lobby. Once they were all out of earshot, Dee turned her back on them and stood close to Tim.

'We've just lied to a policeman,' Dee said. 'Certainly a crime. You sure about this?'

'Eisen— Your granddad told me not to trust

anyone. Your mum doesn't even know about his work.'

'If you're sure. So what now?'

'Well,' Tim said, 'he was staying here because he thought it was safe. Then he goes missing from his room in the middle of the night?'

'What are you saying?'

'It's not safe, is it?' Tim glanced over his shoulder, across the Dawn Star's lobby. 'Someone *here* knows something.'

After they'd gone, Tim asked Elisa if Dee could come for dinner that evening.

'Why?' she said. 'I mean, what will you be doing?'

'Oh, I don't know,' Tim said. 'Just hanging out I suppose. Is it all right? It could be a sleepover?'

'Yes.' Elisa smiled, clearly happy about the idea. It was incredibly rare for Tim to have a friend over, after all. 'It's fine by me.'

It was just after seven o'clock when Dee arrived. She had made Tim promise, and then double promise, not to start investigating without her. Although he

117

had expected to do this alone, he figured she could probably be some use – after all, she knew Eisenstone better than Tim did.

Firstly, however, before they went over all the evidence and their plan, there was one thing to get out of the way.

'Prove it,' Dee said, sitting on the edge of his bed.

'Fine. What do you want?' Tim placed his imagination box on his cabinet.

'I ... I actually need a hairband.' She removed the one she was wearing, showing Tim the lightened threads that had worn thin. 'See.'

'All right,' he said, straightening the hat. 'Colour?'

'In the interest of keeping it unique, and therefore eliminating any elements of trickery, I say make it bright blue, with yellow-and-orange zebra print on the inside, with just a touch of glitter. Throw some polka dots on the outside for good measure.'

'Trickery?' Phil asked. He was sitting on the pillow, stroking his chin.

'Yes,' Dee said, turning to the monkey. 'How can I be sure, unless the hairband is one of a kind?

He could have a hundred hairbands up his sleeve. Sleight of hand. Distraction. There are countless techniques he could use to dupe me.'

'Yes,' Phil said, nodding. 'Quite right. It is important we employ scepticism in the face of such outlandish claims. I too desire proof.'

'Phil, you *are* proof,' Tim said.

'Good point, well made.'

'I just need to witness it myself,' Dee added.

The very moment the box buzzed and started working, Tim could see Dee believed him completely. He stood back, holding his hands up, allowing her to open the lid and see for herself, just as a magician might. The hairband was exactly as she'd ordered. She checked the inside, then put it behind her ears and pushed it on to her head. For a good few seconds, she stared at a spot on the carpet, lost in thought, and no one spoke.

'So,' Phil finally broke the silence, 'who do you suppose would win in a fight between a shark and a bear?'

'Depends entirely on the environment,' Tim said.

'Space station.'

'Well, that seems unlikely but I guess—'

'Give me that hat,' Dee said, standing.

'What, why?' Tim took a step away, holding it on his head.

'Because I want a go.'

'But,' Tim frowned. He felt a strange sense of jealousy. As if Dee was about to read his diary or look through his internet history – he wanted to tell her to get her own, but that seemed both childish and implausible.

'Come on, hand it over.'

Reluctantly, he did as she said and passed the reader to her.

'So, I just imagine what I want, yeah?' The beanie flattened her hair, making it stick out.

'Yes,' Tim said. 'Just picture it as clearly as possible and the box will start working remotely.'

Scrunching her face, she groaned and grimaced and seemed to be in genuine pain. After a minute or so of this troubling display of failure, Tim cleared his throat. 'Are you … finished?' he asked.

'Why isn't anything happening?' she said, pulling the reader off.

'I don't know. Maybe it's because I created it just for me – it's my tailor-made imagination box after all.'

'Right, when I see granddad I'm going to ask – no, *demand* – that he makes me one.'

Although he kind of felt sorry for her, Tim couldn't help but smile with relief. That's why he didn't want to let her try, he realised: he was scared she'd be able to do it.

'All right, enough playing,' Tim said, taking the reader and flinging it on to the bed. 'We've got work to do.'

The three of them went over all the evidence, brainstorming everything they knew so far.

'Right, so we know that Eisenstone didn't arrive in Germany, at least not on the flight he had tickets for,' Tim said. 'He's definitely not at his home – evidence suggests he hasn't been for a while.'

'Mmm,' the monkey replied.

'You said he was talking about feeling watched . . .

stalked,' Dee said, pacing. 'Is it possible that these people have kidnapped him?'

'Perhaps, I suppose, yes,' Tim said. 'Outside the lab, a man in a car took pictures of us – he could have been scouting out his journeys, plotting an abduction?'

'Who was it?'

'I don't know.'

'Professor Eisenstone spoke with some degree of concern about his former partner,' Phil added. 'A connection?'

'Hmm,' Tim agreed. 'Professor Whitelock. The one who died in a fire a few months back ... Maybe his death is linked. Maybe whoever stole his partner's teleporter and burned his lab has targeted Eisenstone. I suppose that would be the key, to find out who else knows about his work, about the imagination box.'

'Is there any way we can get back into his lab,' Dee wondered aloud. 'To see—'

Something shuffled in the vents. Fear swelled inside Tim.

'What the hell was that?!'

'Oh, there it is again,' Tim said, biting his thumbnail and eyeing the stack of books he'd rammed against the grill. 'It's that monster I mentioned.'

'Sorry,' Dee shook her head. 'Remind me again, why did you create it?'

'I didn't *mean* to,' Tim said. 'I used to have this nightmare when I was small. It's silly really. I'm all alone and something is chasing me up some stairs. And when your grandfather said he was leaving, he got me all worried and it came back. Anyway, I fell asleep with the reader on and . . . well, whatever it is that I'm so scared of in the dream it . . . well . . . it escaped. It was an *accident*.'

'Timothy,' Phil said, sitting on his desk. 'Was I an accident?'

'What? No. I told you before, I thought it would be cool to have a finger monkey.'

'Cool? From my research I have concluded that skateboards are cool, IcoRama mobile telephones are cool. Self-aware, talking finger monkeys? Admittedly I am aesthetically quite pleasing,' Phil glanced at himself in the mirror. 'But am I *cool*?'

'I think you're cool. Little talking monkey,' Dee said, 'what's not to like?'

Tim had initially been wary of Dee, but her swift approval of his monkey was tipping the balance in her favour.

Another sound came from the grill in the corner of the room. 'Maybe we should do something about that thing, as it is not at all groovy.' Phil looked worried.

'Like what?' Tim said.

'Maybe we could put a camera in the vents,' he hummed, placing his finger on his furry chin. 'That way, we could watch on your computer to see if it is on its way.'

'That's actually not a bad— Wait. That's it. Phil, you're a genius!' Tim burst into life, grabbing his trainers and pulling them on. Dee stopped pacing and glanced between them.

'Yes, well observed, I am . . . What is the cause of all this energy? Timothy, I find this alarming.'

'Cameras!' Tim shouted.

'Cameras?' Dee looked to Phil.

'Well, yes, of course.' The monkey still looked confused. 'Cameras. Cameras.'

'Elisa put *more* CCTV cameras in the hotel, didn't she? In the hallways. There's one at the end of the corridor now, right outside my door, where I found Eisenstone's watch.'

'They would have recorded what went on that night,' Dee said.

'Exactly.' Tim held his top pocket open. 'Come on, Phil,' he said. 'Not a peep outside my room, remember. We've got to check that footage.'

Within a minute Tim and Dee were upstairs in Elisa and Chris's flat. She was cooking dinner while he was reading the paper at the table.

'All right, guys,' Chris said with a smile. 'What's going on? You having fun?'

'Yes,' Dee said, politely. 'Your hotel is very nice.'

'Oh, we try,' Chris said. 'But it's seen some better days. In fact, some animal-control people are coming tomorrow to look at that pest problem. That woman was pretty shook up. You noticed anything?'

'Nope,' Tim said, glancing at Dee.

'Nothing,' she added.

'She said she'd seen a *monster* in room four ... probably more likely to be a rat, I think.'

'That *is* more likely,' Dee said. 'Statistically.'

'Crossword.' Chris clicked his pen a few times. 'R something, something, S, ten letters. To put back together?'

'Reassemble,' Tim said, instantly.

'Reassemble,' Chris repeated, rushing his pen to the paper. 'All right, how about this one—'

'Chris, we've got—'

'Twelve across. To thoroughly scrutinise for hidden information. Eleven letters.'

'Um ...'

'Something, something, V, E ... unless, of course, six down is wrong, but ...'

Dee laughed quietly to herself. 'Investigate,' she said, smiling.

Tim walked round the table and stood behind Elisa in the kitchen. 'Hey, do you need any help?' he asked.

Still holding a large wooden spoon, she wiped her

forehead with her wrist. 'That's very kind of you, Tim, but I think I have everything under control.'

Relieved she didn't say yes, he asked, 'Elisa . . . you know the CCTV cameras? Are they recording all the time?'

She stopped and looked right at him. He quickly started fiddling with a drawer's handle so he didn't look *too* interested in the answer.

'Um, yes,' Elisa replied, frowning. 'They do record. All the footage is saved on DVDs. It's a very clever system actually – it records and burns it all. Mr Pinkman, he's organising it and he just boxes up the discs, sorts them by date and keeps them in the office. That way, if there's a crime we can just check back.'

'Brilliant!'

'Huh? Yes, it is quite good,' she glanced to her cooking, stirring something in a pot. 'Strange question to ask – why did you want to know?' But when she looked back Tim and Dee had already gone.

They were heading down all five flights of stairs, back to the ground floor.

The lobby was quiet. There was only one guest,

reading a book on the sofa near the windows, and one member of staff at the front desk. They walked straight past the receptionist – she didn't even look up from the computer – into Elisa's office and Tim closed the door gently behind them. Dee homed in on the box marked 'CCTV DVDs', pulling it out across the carpet. Remembering the date they were after, Tim flicked through, arriving in the subsection marked by a piece of handwritten paper: 'Floor two, main hall, camera one'.

'Have you found it yet?' his pocket whispered.

'Phil, shush. You know the rules, no talking outside my room.'

'Noted . . . But have you found it yet?'

'No. I'm after the night he left, August the . . .' Tim fingered through the security discs, systematically noticing every date in its place.

If they could find the right one he could simply watch it and find out what actually happened that night – see what time the professor left and, crucially, if he was alone.

He got to where the DVD should be and stopped.

'That's weird,' Tim whispered.

'What is?' Phil asked. 'Talking to a monkey in your pocket? Or something else?'

'It's not . . . it's . . .' Dee frowned.

'It's missing,' Tim added. 'The DVD of that night is missing, it's gone. All the rest are here but that one has been taken out.'

'What a coincidence,' the monkey mused.

'No, Phil . . . I don't think this is a coincidence.'

Chapter 12

'So,' Dee said the moment they got back to Tim's bedroom. 'What do we know about this Donald Pinkman guy?'

'We know he's in charge of the CCTV, for a start,' Tim said. 'And he's not very nice. But Elisa seems to like him.'

'What's his actual job?' Dee asked.

'He's here temporarily, making the hotel run better. He's a "troubleshooter", a "consultant".'

'A what?'

'Exactly,' Tim said. 'Nonsense. Not a real job at all.'

'Donald Pinkman ... *Donald*,' Dee said. 'It's a silly name too.'

'I believe it is the name of a popular cartoon duck,' Phil added.

'It is,' Tim said. 'That's true. He was asking me about Eisenstone too, when we had tea. And then he told me to keep my nose out of other people's business.'

'Pretty rude, that.' Dee was frowning.

'I assumed he meant stealing cakes and mucking about in the hotel. Maybe he meant something else entirely.'

'Temporary contract? Slight weirdo?' Dee nodded. 'He's sounding like a prime suspect to me.'

'I suggest we find this missing DVD,' the monkey said.

Humming in agreement, Tim paced.

There had been no further sights of the 'deformed monster thing' that the woman from room four insisted was in the vents. However, its intermittent breathing in the walls meant Tim was constantly on edge, always slightly distracted. And when it was silent? He would worry about when it'd next make a noise.

'Right, that's it.' Dee tugged the imagination box

out from under the bed and threw the reader at Tim's chest.

He caught it and then turned to her, confused. 'What? You want something else?'

'Make something,' she demanded. 'Make . . . make a trap. Something. Something that will mean you don't have to think about that thing all day. '

A trap, he thought, not a bad idea. He popped the hat on, and did as she suggested. Carefully Tim moved the books out of the way and slammed his freshly cooked device against the grill as quickly as he could, not risking leaving it open for even a second. The metal contraption covered the vent well and was held in place with magnets.

'There, that should do it,' he said, taking a step back. 'Good old magnets.'

'How does it actually work?' Phil asked, perched on the edge of the bedside cabinet, his tiny feet dangling. It looked a little bit like a small pyramid made from metal.

'Right,' Tim said. 'Inside there is a very clever detection mechanism. When the monster comes near the room, through the vents, it will activate the trap.'

'And then what?' Dee asked.

'When tripped it squirts out loads of extremely quick-setting foam. This should solve the problem quietly.'

'I see,' Phil added. 'But will that not kill the monster?'

'I sincerely hope so.'

'And does this trap have a name?' Phil asked, raising an eyebrow.

'The . . . the Pyramid of Foamy Doom,' Tim said.

'Nice,' Dee gave him a quick thumbs up. 'Right, it's obvious what we've got to do now, isn't it?'

'It is?'

'Yes, we've got to rifle through Donald Pinkman's things,' she said. 'This is the logical next step. Do Dawn Star employees have lockers, anything like that?'

'Um,' Tim thought, 'I don't think so. I've seen him take things from his car though.'

'Let's go.'

After Tim had thrown his brand-new, tailor-made

rucksack on his back and put his reader hat on, they headed downstairs.

Outside in the car park, Dee and Tim, with Phil stowed away in his pocket, strolled as inconspicuously as they could. The shadow of dusk was approaching, the odd street light already on.

'It's the black one,' Tim whispered as they wandered along the line of vehicles. 'It's quite new, not sure of the make though, maybe a Mer— This one.' They came to a stop in front of Donald Pinkman's car. 'Now what?'

Dee stepped fearlessly forwards and tugged on the door handle.

'Woah,' Tim said. 'What are you doing?'

'Trying to open his door?'

'Keep it low-key,' he said.

'Well, it's locked anyway,' Dee shrugged, pressing her face against the passenger window. 'There's nothing in here.'

'What about the back seats?' Tim leant down and cupped his hands around his eyes, feeling the cold glass. 'Oh my.'

'Ding dong!' Phil said, leaning from his pocket and looking inside. 'What's this?'

On the back seat was a book. *The Future of Nanotechnology, Physics in a Quantum World* – by Professor George Eisenstone and Professor Bernard Whitelock.

'He said he's taken a great interest in Eisenstone's work,' Tim said. 'Suspicious.'

One of the changes Donald had suggested, to make the Dawn Star more profitable, was to sort out the top floor. For a long time that level had just been used for storage – there were never guests, just old rooms filled with a maze of furniture and dust. This had meant that Donald spent a lot of his time up there. In fact, he'd commandeered one of the former suites, which he was now using as his office.

The top floors were 'off limits' to Tim. However, prompted by Dee's enthusiasm and their recent discovery, he had decided to ignore Elisa's ban. They headed to the upper storeys at around nine o'clock, after dinner. Donald Pinkman's makeshift office was at the far end of the hall. They walked in tentatively, Tim flicking on the light – it was impeccably clean. He saw a telephone and a computer on the absurdly polished oak desk and a neat pile of paperwork next to the keyboard.

'Weirdo indeed,' Dee said. 'I read somewhere that guilty people are tidy. Makes sense if you think about it.'

Looking out the window Tim could see all the way down to the street below. It was strange how small the cars and tops of lampposts appeared – he could really appreciate how tall the hotel was.

'Yeah ... and why would he want to work all by himself, up here?'

'It could be that he prefers solitude,' Phil suggested.

'Or that he's just a wrong'n,' Dee said.

'But, if he does have something to do with your granddad going missing, then why is he still here?' Tim wondered.

'To keep up appearances.' Dee shrugged, as though it was obvious. 'If he just upped sticks and left, people would definitely suspect something. Anyway, a little less conversation ...'

'What are we actually hoping to find?' Phil wondered. 'Surely, if he did take it, he would have destroyed the DVD?'

'Maybe,' she said. 'But *maybe* not. And if he has, then we'll need to find something else, something concrete.'

The moment Dee grabbed the wooden handle of the desk's top drawer, a door clicked in the hall. Panicked, Tim slammed himself on the ground, shuffling under the desk.

'Dee,' he whispered through clenched teeth. '*Hide.*'

Just as Donald wandered in, she jumped towards the window and wrapped herself in the curtain. Tim heard him step further inside, then saw his legs appear by the chair. There was a deep sigh as he fell into a sitting position. The computer above Tim's head whirred into life and, while it loaded, Donald began drumming with a biro, humming to himself. However, after two beats the pen slipped from his grasp. Tim winced, scrunching his face as it landed on the carpet, right by his knee.

'Whoops-a-daisy,' Donald said to himself. He

pushed his chair back and leant down slowly to retrieve it, his face just coming into view as—

A loud buzz brought him back upright. He answered his mobile and, to Tim's relief, stepped away.

'Hello, yes, not too bad … can … can you hear me?' he said. 'Yes. That's better … no real news yet … yes … the police were here earlier today. They interviewed the boy about the disappearance … no … sorry … it's the signal … hang on a second.' Tim heard Donald leave the room.

'What is happening?' Phil whispered from his pocket.

'Shh.'

Dee emerged from the curtain and crouched. 'Where has he gone?' she asked.

Tim stood and peered down the hall – just in time to see the door to the roof drift closed.

'We've got to follow him,' Dee announced.

'We can't. I'm not allowed up there.'

'You are not allowed on the top floor, but, alas, here we are,' Phil said.

'Yeah, but I'm really, *really*, not allowed on the roof.

I think that rule is actually backed up with reasons – it's dangerous up there.'

'Dangerous?' Dee said. 'How? Just stay away from the edge.'

'I suppose we could.'

'We have to,' she insisted. 'He's talking to someone *right now* about Granddad.'

Tim nodded to himself. 'Fine,' he sighed, shuffling his bag on his back.

All three of them headed with determination down the hallway towards the roof. He arrived at the door, grabbed the handle and cautiously pulled it down. Gently, he tugged – it didn't budge.

'It's locked,' he said, confused. 'Of course, it's on the security latch.'

'Oh. Well that is the end of that then,' Phil said, instantly defeated.

Dee tapped on Tim's head.

'Good thinking.' He closed his eyes and placed his palm on the metal of the lock.

'What is going on now? What are you doing?' Phil asked.

After a few moments of concentrating, he swung his bag off his back, opened up the zip and pulled the lid of his imagination box open. At the bottom of it was a small silver key, with 'Roof' printed on it.

For a brief moment all three gazed down into the opening.

'Goodness me,' Phil said, leaning his head out of Tim's top pocket. 'A key? But you cannot have known the configuration of the lock. This is most amazing.'

'Let's not count our chickens.'

Tim peered at his creation, lifting it closer to his eye – it was drooping, almost melting, as though it was made of clay.

'What?' He was confused. 'That's not how I imagined it.'

'Maybe you're just distracted. Chill out. Make another, but this time out of metal,' Dee suggested.

'Wish I'd thought of that . . .' He pocketed the floppy key and tried again. This time he paid careful attention to the image in his mind. The new one was shiny, glistening – he imagined it cool to touch, heavy in the hand.

Tim grabbed the second key and pushed it into the hole. After his first attempt, he half expected it not to fit. However, it was as though brand new – the mechanism was clean and smooth. The door swung open and a whoosh of fresh air hit them.

'Right, let's be quiet,' Tim whispered, stepping outside.

They headed up the small flight of steel stairs and on to the large, flat roof. Donald was standing on the far side, his back to them. With haste Tim and Dee sneaked around the side, beside some large ventilation boxes, to get close enough to eavesdrop. There were no safety rails, nothing but space between them and the ten-storey fall.

The sunset across Glassbridge's horizon was glowing pink through orange, making silhouettes of a distant flock of birds. Metres away from certain death, Tim didn't pay much attention to the view – he was too busy straining to hear Donald's hushed conversation.

'Yes. Yes,' he was saying softly into his phone. 'Besides all that, things are going very well here …

I had a chat with the child. I think he got the message. He runs around like he owns the place.'

Dee raised an eyebrow at this, but Tim just kept listening, his ears burning red.

'Oh yeah, that,' he continued. 'God knows what that is – something in the vents, probably vermin . . . Well, yes, that too. Obviously it's not good for business if everyone knows people go missing from this place.'

Tim, Dee and Phil all shared a glance.

'I don't think the police have any leads. Obviously for my purposes it'd be better if the professor's disappearance was kept *out* of the public eye. Swept under the rug as best as possible. Would be a disaster to have it linked to the Dawn Star, linked to me. Anyway, I'll keep you posted. Speak soon.' He hung up.

As Donald turned around, as though he could somehow feel he was being watched, Tim dropped lower, hiding. Then the consultant walked slowly to the stairs and back down indoors.

'My God, did you hear that?'

'I heard,' Dee said. 'He wants to keep the disappearance a *secret*?'

'Yes, Timothy, what now?' Phil asked, his arms and head hanging out from the shirt pocket.

Going over everything again, Tim considered the situation. Eisenstone's watch, the missing DVD and now this phone call. Was it enough evidence to prove that Donald was involved in whatever had happened to the professor?

He slipped down to sit cross-legged on the cold gravel, his back against the waist-high ventilation box, which throbbed behind. Dee slouched beside him. Both stared at the last slither of sun disappearing from the sky – long, stretched shadows cut across the roof. After a few seconds he felt the fan inside spin to a stop, fading quietly, but thought nothing of it.

'I think we should tell the police, tell Inspector Kane,' he said, decisively. 'We should pass on everything we know.'

So embroiled was he in this new development that he had forgotten about his nightmare's monster, loose in the hotel's vents. But it had not forgotten about him. The grotesque creature crawled slowly, purposefully on top of the metal directly above their heads. It watched. It waited.

Chapter 13

The beast struggled with six twisted legs, the colour of long-dead flesh with thick black hairs protruding out at various angles. There was one ogling eye on the left side of its 'face'. This monster was truly a creation from the darkest places inside Tim. The makings of a nightmare.

'Without concrete evidence, what will Inspector Kane do though?' Phil asked.

'I don't know,' Tim said, biting his thumb and staring across the roof. 'Take him in for questioning?'

A long streak of drool trailed out of the animal's mouth, glistening in the warm dusk light.

'That's my vote,' Dee said. 'We go straight to the police. That's the rational reaction to this. Whatever mess Granddad is in, we've got to sort it out.'

'Yes, fine, we'll go and—'

The spit landed on Tim's shoulder and ran down his arm. 'What?' Confused, he very slowly turned, desperate not to see what he thought he might.

Inches from his face the monster hissed. Scrambling to his feet, shaking, he shuffled backwards, turning his head in terror.

Dee was yet to notice. She stood, frowning. 'Tim, are you all right?'

Clueless as to what it would do, he held his hands up. The only thing that saved Tim in his horrible dreams was the realisation that it was, in fact, a dream. Here though, in the real world, he didn't have this safety net. There was no escaping. He could *not* wake up.

It leapt on to the ground, sending several pieces of gravel flying as it growled again. Dee's body tensed as she finally turned to look at the creature.

'Oh, what is *that*?' she said, stepping back.

Holding itself up to its full height on its stunted legs, it seemed almost proud of the fact that it had joined Tim in the real world where it could truly

146

terrorise him. Like a rabid dog, snarling and snapping, it advanced. Its joints clicked and squelched as it jerked along.

'Um,' Dee said, throwing her arms into the air. 'Suggestions? Tim? What shall I do?' There was no response. 'I feel I should kick it, but I don't want to.'

Phil's head emerged from Tim's pocket. 'Oh, that is just ghastly. What the . . . Good grief.'

It occurred to Tim that this was not a perfect model of his dark vision. It was poorly constructed – created during sleep. This *somehow* made it worse. He staggered backwards, his heart hit the inside of his ribcage, over and over, so hard he could feel it in his neck.

Scurrying side to side, it let out a haunting, throaty gurgle.

'All right, this is a bit much,' Dee said. 'I'm going to get help.' She turned and ran across the roof, back towards the stairs.

There was less than a metre between Tim and the edge.

'Timothy, stop. The edge.' Phil was now yelling.

He climbed from his pocket on to Tim's shoulder, tugging on his collar. 'Stop.'

But all Tim could do was retreat. Gripped in the tightest hold by fear, he couldn't think beyond moving away. His heels were now flush with the end of the building. Tiny pieces of dust and gravel crumbled off the roof, falling fast to the ground where they disappeared out of sight.

There was a stand-off.

'It's ... stopped ... What ... what does it want?' Tim whimpered.

He finally turned, spotting how close to the fall he was, and as he did so the monster let out a screech, louder than any before. The sound shook Tim to his core – he swayed, losing his balance, and his left foot slipped off behind him. Instinctively, he threw his weight forwards as he fell.

Thumping on to the roof, he landed, winded, on his front. Now level with the beast, he felt both his legs go. In less than a second, his weight shifted more and more towards death and away from safety. The guttering bent at his stomach.

Phil scurried to his hand where he started nobly pulling on his sleeve, but it proved useless. Tim's fingers scrambled, desperately searching for something to grab on to. He slipped out a little, his forearm resting now on the wilting gutter – his legs frantically kicked below him, flailing in the thin air. The monster came near, its breath on his hair, almost making contact – he closed his eyes and waited. But it turned, cowering, and crawled away, back to its vents. Where was it going? It had him at his mercy. Why was it retreating now?

With a deep breath Tim tried to swing himself back up, but the gutter broke. He fell a little further – bashing his chin – and was now hanging from just his fingers, with ten floors of nothing below him.

'Tim?' called a voice from above. It was Dee. 'Uh, Tim? Where are you?'

'I'm here! Follow the sound of my voice,' he groaned.

Her head appeared above him, next to Phil's, her hair hanging down as she leant over. 'I went to get help, but the door is locked.'

'Of course it is,' Tim sighed. 'Pull me up.'

She lay down flat and grabbed his arm, tugging with what felt like a feeble amount of effort. He barely moved. 'You're too heavy.'

'No, you're just not strong enough.'

'What a pickle,' Phil added.

Twisting his weight from raw panic caused a screw to ping off above and Tim lowered another metre or so, bouncing to a stop. Now dangling from a vertical, disconnected bit of metal, there was only a single, very rusty bracket keeping him alive.

'Right, well, I am going to die,' Tim said, his hands sliding, arms burning. 'It's as simple as that.'

'No!' Dee yelled. 'Make something, anything!'

'Gah, all right.' Tim scrunched his face, trying desperately to imagine a way out of this situation, thinking hard over the distracting circumstances. His numb grip now unreliable.

'Come along,' Phil yelled. 'Faster.'

'You know, that doesn't actually help me concentrate.'

Tim closed his eyes again. 'Done!' he said. 'Quickly, climb down me, Phil.'

The monkey leapt on to his shoulder, then on to the bag where he tugged the zip open. 'What in heaven's name is this?' he said, peering into the imagination box.

'Pass me the controls,' Tim ordered. There was no time to explain. He held on with his right hand, and waved his left hand about behind him until he felt the hard plastic of the remote control pressed into his palm. Hastily he put it in his mouth. Again, he reached into his bag, over his shoulder, and yanked a small jetpack out. It had straps and a handle.

'Is that a . . . jetpack?' Dee asked, in a high-pitched voice.

'Yes. Now, let me just—'

The guttering snapped – they fell – the roof disappearing above.

Tim clawed at his invention, fumbling for the right buttons as he and Phil dropped through the howling air.

In a blink they were nearly at the ground as the jetpack erupted in Tim's hand – bright, spewing flame and smoke, slowing them, and then lifting them away from the building, wildly spinning.

Clinging on to the edge of the makeshift machine, Tim, for a moment, seemed to have control. They flew awesomely into the air, in grand circles. The wind flowed through his clothes, now in the opposite direction. They were *actually* flying. But then they flew straight into the side of the hotel.

They smashed head first into a window a few storeys up, before bumping down the bricks – fire and vapour still bellowing out of the contraption. Near the ground they spun upside down, drifting out a bit, before Tim let go.

He landed with a savage thud next to the piece of gutter, followed by Phil, followed by the jetpack – *smash* – followed by the imagination box – *whack* – all strung out on the pavement. After a sputter, the jetpack fired up by itself, spiralling off at great speed along the ground, leaving a foggy trail, before wedging itself under the wheel arch of a parked car. The heat blasted from the back of it for a second, and then it sparked, fizzled and seemed to stop.

'Ouch,' Tim said, glancing around, still lying on his back. A new appreciation for solid ground washed over him as he stroked the cold concrete.

He was safe.

'That was … stressful,' Tim said, coughing. He looked up to see Dee's tiny head. Her hand came out – she waved and gave him a thumbs up.

'Maybe you should listen to Elisa?' Phil said, clambering on to Tim's chest.

'Yes, I agree, the roof is, quite rightly, off limits.'

'You know, I think Dee meant make a rope or something of that nature.'

'Yeah,' Tim croaked, propped up on his elbow. 'Maybe, in hindsight, that would have been better, but it still got us down safely.'

'Just.'

'And it's an all-right creation I think, all things considered.'

The jetpack exploded under the car, blowing glass and fire on to nearby vehicles. A symphony of alarms kicked off as the thick black smoke, filled with fresh embers, rose up into the sky.

Phil's eyes bulged at the surprisingly large flames. 'Shall we go indoors?'

'Yes please.'

Chapter 14

Tim and Dee got up early to head to the police station. They had toyed with the idea of calling the police the night before, but Eisenstone's warnings about trusting no one held them back. They needed to speak with Inspector Kane – no one else would do. Tim put everything on: his red-chequered shirt, hat and rucksack. It had become routine that he'd take the imagination box with him wherever he went – in fact, he felt naked without it. The station wasn't far from the hotel – Tim, Dee and Phil crossed Glassbridge's large park, cut a diagonal path up the busy high street and arrived within fifteen minutes.

On their way out Tim had told Elisa that they were going to speak with Inspector Kane about something he had remembered from the night of Eisenstone's disappearance. It was kind of a lie, but kind of true. (They decided it was too premature to tell her about what they'd discovered. In fact, Tim imagined she'd tell him to 'stop being silly' if he started accusing Donald Pinkman of any wrongdoing.)

'Funnily enough, you just missed the police,' she had said. 'Someone broke a window and started a fire in the car park last night, you must have heard a bang?'

'We were fast asleep,' Tim said.

'Like a pair of babies,' Dee added. 'Drunk ones.'

This lie was necessary – Tim wouldn't even know where to start if he was forced to tell the truth. If he had simply said that it was his imagined jetpack that blew up under the car Elisa would have invariably probed him further. That kind of information couldn't be digested by most people without a lengthy conversation.

The previous night they had managed to slip into the hotel as people rushed out to see what all the noise was. He got upstairs and opened the roof door for Dee without anyone spotting him. They then went straight to bed. Tim had his lies poised, his excuses ready.

Luckily, there was no knock at the door.

The police station's reception smelled like school: paper, pencils and faintly warm plastic from the computer. The lady at the desk fetched Inspector Kane, who smiled when he spotted them both.

'Ah, Dee, Tim, come on through,' the policeman said. Kane waddled as he walked down the long corridor. The floor was shiny and green, like a sports hall, with odd black rubber scuffs. They arrived in Kane's office, where the inspector checked up and down the corridor before closing the door.

'Please, sit,' he said, pointing at a couple of chairs.

Kane moved his body round the desk and sat on his slightly higher swivel chair, directly opposite. 'So, what can I do for you today?'

'Well, it's about Professor Eisenstone. Since he went missing we—'

'There are inquiries being made – he's not been declared missing *officially*, but carry on,' Kane said.

He picked up his mug of coffee and began taking a swig.

'We think Donald Pinkman might know something about it,' Tim said.

Inspector Kane stopped, with his cup in his mouth, and took a good couple of seconds before he swallowed his coffee.

'Right.' He placed his mug carefully on the coaster. 'Why do you think that?'

'He's working at the Dawn Star Hotel,' Tim said. 'As a consultant, as you know. Anyway, he started not long before Eisenstone went . . .'

'I see.' Inspector Kane leant back on his chair and pulled out a notepad from his top drawer.

'And . . . Well, we think he might know something about it. I think you should speak to him again.'

Slowly shaking his head, Kane clicked his pen a few times. 'Hmm. What, exactly, are you basing this on? You can't just go round making accusations.'

They then explained what they'd discovered – the missing CCTV footage and the fact that Donald had access to the DVDs.

'I'm afraid this is flimsy evidence, Tim, as interesting as it is,' Kane answered.

'We heard him talk about Granddad on the telephone.' Dee tapped the table with her finger. 'He mentioned him by name. He said it would be best if the disappearance was kept quiet.'

Inspector Kane sighed. 'Well, it would look bad for the Dawn Star I suppose. I've spoken to Mr Pinkman – he works for a consultancy firm, he was probably checking in with his organisation. Look, people talk about people all the time on the phone. The man is well known, he might be missing, there are thousands of reasons he could be speaking about him. We're speaking about him now – are any of us guilty?'

'And he told me . . . he told me to keep my nose out of other people's . . . business . . .' Tim deflated – all of a sudden he was full of doubt, wondering whether there could be an innocent explanation for all he'd seen.

'Listen –,' Kane placed his pen on his pad – 'I admire your enthusiasm, but I fear you are maybe letting your imagination run wild.'

Tim couldn't help but smile. 'But . . .'

'OK,' Kane said, firmly. 'It's *our* job to find Professor Eisenstone. If there is any wrongdoing, rest assured, we'll get to the bottom of it.'

'I . . . it's just . . .' Tim struggled to find the words. He was annoyed that Inspector Kane wasn't taking his theory more seriously. Perhaps if he knew the importance of the contraption . . .

'His work,' Dee said, clearly thinking the same thing. 'It was very . . .'

'What do you know about his work?'

Eisenstone's words echoed in Tim's mind. He gave Dee the slightest of head shakes.

'I don't know anything much really,' she said. 'But he told me it is . . . important.'

Kane's interest dispersed and his chair creaked as he reclined. 'I'm sure it was. Now I urge you, as a police officer and as a friend, to stop this. It's not a good idea to carry on snooping around. There is a process and anything you do could interfere with that.'

Tim nodded, but he wasn't really listening – his

mind was spinning, possible explanations flashing and bouncing around in his head. He needed answers.

Initially, the meeting with Inspector Kane took the wind out of their sails. But the moment Tim and Dee got to the hotel, they picked up where they left off – looking for some harder evidence. They knew they needed something concrete to make the policeman take notice.

Much later, sitting at his desk, a little after 3.30 a.m., Tim rubbed his temples in gentle circles. The lamp made an oasis, a warm yellow bubble in the cold of night where he thought of only one thing: Professor Eisenstone.

Dee had convinced her mum to let her stay another night. They both stared down at his sketch pad. The whole case – all his notes, were scribbled messily on the paper, bordered by various sketches, some of random patterns and some of Phil. He had half drawn a picture of his nightmare monster, but had since scribbled it out. It was still at large, still tormenting him from the vents.

They'd talked at great length about where to take their investigation next. Both had agreed, and Tim circled the final bullet point: 'Eisenstone's former partner'.

'Professor Bernard Whitelock,' Tim said. 'He worked with Eisenstone but died a couple of months back. He helped design the imagination box. It seems that Professor Eisenstone, Professor Whitelock, me and now you are the only people we can be *sure* have ever known about it ... Who is Professor Whitelock?'

'I met him once or twice when I was small,' Dee said. 'But I know that something happened between them – I think something with their work. Granddad never really spoke about it. Either way, they weren't close towards the end.'

They spent the next hour searching the name, and every variation, online. They'd done this before, but had only had a cursory glance. Now though, they decided to dedicate some real time to researching Whitelock. They read some of his papers on nanotechnology, most of which were incredibly technical. There were no clues. Tim found an article in some obscure academic journal about Professor Eisenstone and Professor Whitelock. There was a photo of them both, posing in a lab. Eisenstone didn't look much different, besides having slightly more hair and it being thicker and brown.

The last site they read was an obituary. It was all about Professor Whitelock, his work and his 'tragic death'. It didn't mention his troubled final years that Eisenstone spoke of. In fact it just seemed to praise the man as a genius. Tim read the final paragraph, his chin resting on his hand:

'The untimely death of this great man was a shock to the academic community as much as to friends and family. Professor Bernard Whitelock leaves his wife, whom he married just months prior to his death, former Glassbridge MP, Clarice Crowfield. His contribution to scientific advancement is indisputable; his work has paved the way for—'

Bolt upright now, Tim turned to Dee, who leant closer to his screen. He shook his head and reread the last sentence.

Their attention, in unison, fell on the name Clarice Crowfield.

Professor Whitelock married Clarice *Crowfield* before he died.

Tim had thought it when he first met the new chef, and he thought it once again: Crowfield was not a common name.

Chapter 15

'Stephen Crowfield . . . the new chef,' Tim said, still sitting at his desk, taking it all in. 'This is it. This is the connection.'

Dee explained, in her ever-rational way, that more evidence was required. 'This could still be a spurious correlation,' she said, fist on her bottom lip.

'A whaty what?'

'A spurious correlation is when two things appear to be linked, but in fact are not,' she said. 'It pains me to say it, but Inspector Kane might have had a point. We can't let our imaginations guide us any further. We need to head down to fact town.'

She was right. They had to be sure. 'What have you got in mind?' he asked.

'Is there a record of when Dawn Star staff work?'

'Um,' Tim nodded. 'Yeah, there must be. The rotas.'

'Where are they or, more specifically, where is Stephen's?'

'His will be at the workstation at the back of the kitchen, I imagine.'

'We could look at it, find out if he was here on the night before Granddad's flight?'

'Let's go.'

Tim hadn't even realised the time until they stepped out of his bedroom. The hotel was dead, silent. Straight down the stairs, through the hall – no time for lava – to the lobby, which was completely empty besides the night porter, who was slumped, reading a magazine at reception. He didn't notice them briskly pass through and to the kitchen doors.

'Down here,' Tim said, pointing ahead of them.

It was weird seeing this place – usually bristling with commotion and heat – in a quiet and cold state. Everything seemed grey. At the back of the room, behind a dividing wall, was a messy desk. Tim switched on the lamp and, without another word, Dee began searching through the drawers.

'This it?' she said, holding up a folder.

'Looks like it.'

With a lick of her thumb, she flicked through the staff rota, scanning down the column marked 'S. Crowfield', noticing the days the young chef had filed overtime. There was just one single evening he'd worked late: the night Professor Eisenstone went missing.

'That's it,' Tim said, placing his finger on the entry, then tapping it. 'And look . . . he's not down to work from next week onwards.'

'Maybe he's resigned?' Dee wondered. 'Maybe his job is done.' With that, she returned the folder to the third drawer down. 'We should leave it as we found it. We don't want to arouse— Wow. What's this?!'

She slid a plastic DVD case out from under some pens and clutter. Tim removed the disc and inspected it. Something on the front had been scribbled over with black marker – he flipped it over to see that the back was scratched. There were deep grooves across the rainbow silver.

'This has got to be the footage of that night,' Tim said. 'Whatever is on here, Stephen doesn't want the world to see . . .'

'Why hasn't he got rid of it completely – he's not very good at this, is he?'

'Careless. Right.' Tim turned the lamp off and pocketed the DVD. 'They can still recover data from these things.'

Walking briskly from the kitchen, Dee whispered from behind, 'We need to confirm Stephen and Clarice are definitely related.'

'Crowfield is a pretty rare name,' Tim said quietly over his shoulder.

'I know, but we've got to be certain.'

'How?'

'We could look up his address, his number?' Dee suggested. 'We could ring and literally ask for Clarice.'

'That's just—'

'So simple, bold and logical it makes complete sense?' Dee smiled. 'Why thank you.'

They paused at the edge of the dining hall, before rounding the corner and heading back into reception. 'We'll need to look on Elisa's computer,' Tim said, peering at the night porter. 'Which means getting rid of him.'

'Hmm.' Dee turned to look at the phone on the wall by their side, used by waiting staff to take table bookings for the restaurant. She picked it up – the tone hummed gently. 'How do you call reception?'

'Um, press nine and then press the hash key.'

She hit the buttons and, still hidden behind the corner, twirled the curly wire as she spoke in a very strange, posh voice. 'Ah, yes, hello there,' she said to the porter. Tim couldn't help but snigger. 'My name is Francesca Bumblesnatch. I am staying in room thirty and I think there's a burst pipe in the hallway. There's a terrific puddle of water. I suggest you come right away.'

'Oh, thanks for letting me know. I will check it out,' the porter said.

With him gone, they swept to the office behind reception and logged straight on to the computer.

Once the monitor was on, he clicked to the staff folder on the desktop, opened it up and took down the chef's home number. He noticed his address was Crowfield House.

Back in his room, and spurred on by Dee, he dialled, not giving a thought to how late it was. After a few rings, a flustered woman answered.

'Yes, hello,' she said in an angry, tired voice. 'Do you know what time it is?'

'What is your name?' Tim asked. Dee gave him a firm thumbs up – clearly pleased with how direct he was being.

'*You* rang *me*. You know perfectly well that I am Clarice Crowfield and—'

Tim hung up. 'Right,' he said. 'Stephen lives with Clarice.'

'And that was her name when she married Professor Whitelock,' Dee said.

'So . . .'

'It's probably her maiden name. So she's not Stephen's wife. Got to be a relative. Sister? Mother?'

'She sounded old.'

'Mother then.'

'We need to speak with Inspector Kane,' Tim said. 'We can't trust anyone else.'

'So we've got to wait until the station opens?' Dee shook her head. 'No way. Stephen's done *something*. Whatever is on the DVD is obviously incriminating. What if they've taken Granddad? Or worse. Plus, what if Inspector Kane *still* doesn't think this is enough to investigate? You saw how reluctant he was to do anything – he thought we were speaking nonsense.'

'Well, what are you suggesting?'

'I think we should go there, to their house, and have a look about,' Dee said. 'Get some concrete evidence.'

'When?' Tim asked. 'Now?'

A moment later and Dee was zipping up her jacket and slipping on her shoes. Tim tied his laces, stood and finally placed his reader hat on in front of the mirror. Dressed in a dark, maroon-chequered shirt, he tightened the straps on his rucksack. He was ready.

Tim pulled open the top drawer to see Phil tucked

up peacefully in his perfectly made miniature bed. 'Phil, wake up,' Tim said.

'What in heaven's name? What time is it?' the monkey mumbled.

'I don't know – a million o'clock? We're going out. Do you want to come?'

'Pardon? Where? It is still dark.'

'We're going to Crowfield House.'

'I beg your pardon, Timothy?'

'We've had some breakthroughs – we need to look in Stephen Crowfield's home.' Tim then explained what they had learned.

'You plan to break in?' Phil asked, standing.

'Don't make it sound like *we're* the baddies,' Tim said. 'But yes.'

'We have just cause, Phil,' Dee added. 'This is all very reasonable.'

She swung her coat's hood on to her head – in the shadow Tim could still see the white polka dots on the hairband he'd made for her.

'What about Elisa?' The monkey was concerned, as Tim knew he *should* have been.

For some reason he just couldn't find anywhere in his head that worried about the consequences. He thought for a moment about the morning he met Eisenstone – the stolen cakes. What a tame crime it was, and now he was preparing to leave in the dead of night to break into someone's house.

'Elisa won't mind,' Tim said. 'She won't find out.'

'Hmm, is this not a trifle . . . illegal?'

'Certainly,' Dee said. 'But, like, literally, what's the worst that could happen?'

'Prison?' the monkey suggested.

'For breaking into someone's home? No,' Dee said. 'Children rarely go to prison. Especially not for something minor. I think this kind of thing is *frowned upon*, sure, but legal consequences? Pfft, unlikely.'

'I am afraid I am still a little apprehensive,' Phil added

'Look,' Tim sighed. 'Clarice Crowfield, who lives with Stephen Crowfield at Crowfield House – the old mental home on the hill – married *Professor Whitelock*. Remember, Eisenstone's old colleague, who died?'

'OK. I am following so far.'

'I think Clarice Crowfield knows something about the imagination box, about Eisenstone's work. Firstly, the watch is enough reason to be sure that the professor is missing. We've checked everywhere he should be. He's gone. The destroyed CCTV footage, the fact that Stephen Crowfield has concrete links to the *only* other living soul we can be *sure* knew about Eisenstone's invention, *and* he was working here the very night the professor disappeared. Don't you get it, Phil? It all adds up.'

'Totally fits together,' Dee agreed. 'Tim's right. Plus, Inspector Kane won't listen until we have something absolute. We need proof.'

'Yes,' Tim said. 'You took the words right out of my mouth. Now, it could be risky, it could be dangerous. You don't have to join us if you don't want to – I will completely understand if you'd—'

'Worry not, old bean, I am coming.'

Chapter 16

The first embers of the morning sun were just appearing in the sky, but pre-dawn blueness still covered everything in sight. Tim, Dee and Phil made short work of the trek across Glassbridge and up Chestnut Hill, to the highest point in town.

Having jogged most of the way, they slowed to a walking pace quite a long distance from their target. Ivy, much of which was dried on to the crumbling bricks, climbed up and over the perimeter wall. The gate had grand, curly fittings at the top, with 'Crowfield House' spelled out in fancy writing cast from iron. They stood at the entrance, looked through the bars and watched the building for a few moments.

There wasn't a single glowing window. This was

good news; if everyone was asleep it would make their break-in easier. There was still no doubt in Tim's mind, no fear and no suggestions that they should turn back. Some of the grey wall was broken, with some cracked bricks halfway up. Tim found his footing and scrambled up and over. Landing on damp grass on the other side, he stood and wiped his hands on his jeans. It was there he had his first shimmer of worry. Besides the bus fair, this trespass was the first real crime Tim had ever committed (he decided that the jetpack explosion didn't count because that was a genuine accident).

Dee fell behind him, just keeping her balance.

'You ... you sure about this?' he whispered, swallowing.

'No,' Phil said from his pocket.

'Well,' she shrugged, brushing herself off, 'we've come this far.'

The turf was soft under foot. They made sure not to step on the tarmac path that led up to the driveway and, after a short walk, made it to the side of the house. He had planned to quickly create a key, but saw that the back door was boarded up with wood and nails.

'Looks like they're trying to keep people out,' Tim said, rubbing his hand across one of the planks.

'Or keep someone *in*,' Dee suggested.

Crowfield House was huge, imposing and, Tim couldn't help but admit, scary. It looked as though it had been abandoned years ago, with overgrown foliage and peeling paintwork. Above them was an open window. On their left was a wooden trellis with crinkled, dead plants clinging on to it. Tim tugged, making sure it was sturdy. When they decided it could safely hold their weight, Dee began climbing and, at the top, passed her legs over the windowsill.

'Shh,' she said, helping Tim in.

His vision adjusted to the new light and, realising he was in a bedroom, his eyes snapped to the bed. It was empty. They moved silently but, a few steps in, there was an incredibly loud creak from a floorboard beneath the carpet. Sweat prickled up his back as he carefully lifted his foot. As slowly as humanly possible, Dee opened the door and they passed through into the hall. Tim was shaking as they crept through the house, to the stairs, where he saw the grand entrance, from the inside. A sudden wash of new panic hit him.

He grabbed Dee by the arm. 'What if they've got a dog?!' he whispered.

'Then I imagine it'll probably bark in the next few seconds,' she said, stepping on to the first step.

The search of the ground floor was fairly quick and luckily there were no pets to give them away. There was some unusual antique furniture, but none of the concrete evidence they had hoped to find. Until, that is, they arrived in the study.

This was by far the largest room they'd come across. It had floor-to-ceiling bookcases and a wide desk in front of two long windows covered with thick velvet curtains.

The first thing Tim noticed was the huge, imposing painting of a woman on the wall. A small silver plaque at the base read: 'Clarice Crowfield'. Wearing a posh suit and a set of gold mayor's chains, she watched over the study, constantly maintaining eye contact with them wherever they moved. Below, pinned on the wall, there were countless newspaper clippings and photographs. Headlines proclaimed her a 'rising star', and black-and-white snapshots showed her shaking hands with important public figures, some of whom were familiar to Tim. He thought it strange that she'd have such a dominant portrait of herself.

'Do you recognise this woman?' Tim asked.

'Nope.'

A little further along was a stuffed owl, perched on a polished wooden pedestal in the corner, which also watched over them, its glassy eyes glistening like this year's pennies.

And then they spotted it.

On large noticeboards, mounted on a few artists' easels, was a sea of evidence. Although this is what they'd hoped to find, the discovery made Tim's heart sink. The Crowfields were extremely guilty. There were countless photos of Eisenstone, with Post-it notes and biro arrows linking scribbles to one another. Tim's fear ramped up a gear when he spotted pictures of himself. Some were of him entering the lab with the professor and getting in and out of his car, confirming again what he thought he'd seen. There were notes bordering an early blueprint of the first imagination box prototype. It was a detailed sketch that had obviously been stolen. Every part of it was labelled with thick blocks of text.

'Look,' Tim whispered.

'They nicked all of this,' Dee added, lifting her brow. 'Cheeky freaks.'

'This is enough – let us go,' Phil said.

'No, wait a second.' Tim stepped closer to the collage of evidence. 'Look, they've got Eisenstone's notes that he was making with me. It says what he'd created. A sausage, a marble, *a finger monkey* – they know everything.'

'Really? Oh. We should definitely leave.' Phil wriggled in Tim's top pocket.

'Check this out,' Dee said.

On one of the boards was the date of the professor's flight to Germany, with 'Abducting the information' written beneath.

'Wait, can you feel that?' Tim said.

'Feel what?' Phil replied.

'A draught.'

They followed the cold air. It brought them to one of the bookcases across from the desk. Dee licked her thumb and held it at the edge of the wood, between two sets of shelves.

'It's coming from here,' she said, craning her neck. 'This is a door.'

With the tips of his fingers Tim tugged at the small gap, trying to get the case to move. It was no use. He stepped back, defeated.

'Maybe not?' Phil said.

'Or perhaps there's a secret button or something?' Tim replied as he started inspecting each shelf. 'If they've got all that stuff in plain view, just *imagine* what they'd want to hide.'

Dee began pushing loose books around, looking at the shelf behind them, but one of them didn't budge – it was fixed. Tim and Dee shared a smile.

Slowly she pulled the book down towards them. A low clunk followed by a hiss and the shelf pushed out into the room. Dee got her hand behind it and tugged the heavy door open enough for them to slip inside the secret passage. The air was damp and the stone walls radiated a chill. Pitch black.

'I can't see a thing,' she whispered, her voice almost silent.

The familiar sound of the imagination box working echoed in the darkness and then, about ten seconds later, the space lit up and Tim had a torch in his hand.

'Ta da,' he said as the tunnel appeared in front of them.

A handle at the far end glistened in the light. They headed down the long, spacious corridor and Tim pushed the door open.

Inside, they were greeted by the sight of a huge, cluttered laboratory. The torch beam picked up the floating dust that explored the still air. The place looked expensive but neglected. Only one or two worktables were clear – the others were piled with old junk. One shelf had nothing but electrical equipment on it, dangling wires and circuit boards jutting out at all angles. Their eyes followed the light as he swept it round to the right-hand end of the room. Two large metal chambers, the size of coffins, stood side by side, connected by thick wads of cables. Each had a small glass window in the centre – they looked like something you'd find on a submarine.

'Look at this,' Tim whispered.

'What is it?' Dee squinted.

They went closer. Tim felt cool air cling to his clothes. 'It's a teleporter,' he announced, lighting up one of the cylinders.

'How can you be so sure?' Phil asked. 'It is just two metal things. It could be absolutely anything. You must remember never to assume, Timothy.'

'It says "teleporter" on it,' Tim replied.

The torch beam fell on the bottom of the control box between the two chambers. It did, in fact, say 'teleporter' on the side, followed by lots of numbers.

'Oh yes. So it does,' Phil admitted.

'Do you think this is Professor Whitelock's?' Dee whispered. 'You said someone stole his teleporter? But this is his wife's house . . . Why would she—'

A creak came from somewhere in the building. They all froze. Tim clicked the torch off and placed his hand on Dee's shoulder. All he could hear was their tightened breathing and his own thrumming pulse between his ears.

'Timothy,' Phil finally whispered, his voice trembling. 'I am experiencing the physiological symptoms of fear. It does not feel good.'

The light came back on. 'All right,' Tim croaked, over his heartbeat. 'Maybe it is time to leave.'

They turned but, at the opposite end of the lab was another huge chamber, the size of a separate room.

'Hang on,' Tim whispered, walking briskly across the flat concrete.

He and Dee inspected it for some time, before he realised what the machine was.

'Do you know what *this* is?' Tim said, peering in through one of its windows. It was empty. 'I think it's an imagination box.'

'It's gigantic.' Dee looked up – it reached the high ceiling.

'Yes,' Tim said. 'It's a lot like your grandfather's prototype, only much bigger. But the reader is . . .' Tim glanced around near the control box.

He followed the wires, finding empty plugs on the end. Then on a workbench against the wall, he spotted the reader connected to a laptop.

'Look at this,' Tim said, picking it up. It was heavy, covered in complex components, and surely very uncomfortable to wear. It reminded him of a weird fighter pilot's helmet. 'Why is it plugged into the computer though?'

He pressed a key on the laptop and it lit up instantly, having been dormant on standby. On the desktop was a folder marked 'Reading Tests'. Tim double-clicked it.

A groan emanated from the building – maybe a pipe – and Tim hesitated.

'The sensation is intensifying,' Phil added. 'I think our departure should be prioritised.'

'In a minute,' Dee said, stepping forwards and looking down at the screen. There was a subfolder marked 'Eisenstone'. She moved Tim's dawdling hands away and clicked it open herself. It was empty. Back into the main folder she selected 'Stephen's Tests'. There was one file, called 'Thought Read 1'.

'Stephen's tests?' Tim wondered.

The screen went blank, then colours and code spread across it, shapes and words, letters, numbers, symbols, abstract blobs – it was random nonsense. Then a picture of a thin, black-haired woman began to emerge, firstly as juddering digital squares, and then clear as day. Clarice Crowfield. It was like footage from an old film, jumping and cutting roughly. Sometimes it rewound, sometimes it broke up and disappeared under smudges and lines.

She appeared to be happy, smart, young and glowing, like she had been in that painting. She twirled in the sunlight, smiled into a mirror and played tea-towel peek-a-boo with the 'camera', looking directly back at Tim through the screen. But then the image morphed, colour drained, and she was screaming about something – all from Stephen's point of view.

'These are memories,' Tim said. 'This is what the reader has taken from Stephen's head. It must translate thoughts into . . . this.'

A jumpy cut produced another memory. Early morning, a kitchen window. A quick cut to Stephen, again from a low perspective, a child's perspective, wandering up the hall. He was carrying a tray of what looked like a freshly made breakfast – pancakes, fruit, a glass of orange juice, all spread out beautifully. Even a flower in a small vase. It went blurry and fuzzy, and then he arrived in Clarice's bedroom. She woke, frowning. Then some shouting. A flash to the breakfast on the floor, smashed glass and ruined food, back up to Clarice who was shaking her head. Tim lip-read, 'Rubbish – absolute rubbish'.

Other memories played out: blurred colours and ripples and then Clarice was shouting, pointing, throwing things. 'It's your fault,' she whispered, through tight lips. 'I had so much potential, stolen, by you. Think of what I could have done.' Stephen's childhood had clearly been no treat – it seemed his mother placed the blame for all her failings at his feet.

Then it leapt forwards once more. Clarice stood over Stephen as he filled in an application form with the Dawn Star logo on top. They saw the hotel, as Stephen saw it – it was brighter, somehow nicer than the reality. It was obvious he liked it – the memory was happy, positive, unlike those that featured his mother.

Tim saw himself, saw that Stephen had been spying – taking pictures, keeping watch. The footage flickered again though, all the colour faded and Eisenstone appeared. Stephen's hands crumbled pills, white tablets, into a drink.

A few more frantic distortions gradually slowed down. The word 'sorry' appeared again, scrolling and rolling around on the screen, sometimes on paper, sometimes just floating through the air like smoke in a breeze.

'My goodness,' Phil said.

'It was all her. Clarice put him up to it ... Poor Stephen.' Tim closed the laptop lid. 'I can't watch that any more.'

'They are using the reader to *look* at thoughts,' Dee said, astonished.

'If you think about it, that's what readers are doing – maybe this is just displaying them, rather than creating them?'

'It is amazing,' Phil added. 'To extract memories. And the empty folder? Is that what they are doing with Professor Eisenstone?'

'Maybe,' Tim replied, still disturbed by the visions of Stephen Crowfield's dark past. 'Maybe these memories are just an experiment. Perhaps they want to read the professor's mind to find out how he made *his* imagination box work?'

'So if that means they *have* kidnapped him,' Dee concluded. 'Then . . . where is he?'

Back in the study, Tim gently closed the door to the secret passageway behind them. It felt like they'd been in there a while, the early-morning sun was now coming through the slit between the long curtains. Stephen's recorded memories had showed that he'd drugged and, most likely, kidnapped Eisenstone, all under the instruction of his mother. They'd been using the reader from their huge imagination box to do what the device did best – read minds. Clarice was obviously carrying on with Whitelock's work but, Tim suspected, wasn't particularly successful.

Sneaking, they went back to the boards covered with photos and notes. This was enough. This was the evidence they needed.

'Right,' he said, pulling the imagination box from his rucksack. He thought hard of a digital camera, compact, efficient and high resolution.

'What is *that*?' Dee whispered, as the lid slid open to reveal his creation.

Tim grumbled to himself as he pulled a postcard from the contraption – it had a *photo* of a camera on the front.

'It is a lovely picture,' Phil said.

'All right, everyone be quiet.' Again, Tim tried. This time he crouched, gently rubbing the sides of his head, trying to remain calm, ignoring the fact he was halfway through a break-in. Imagining the intricate electronics, the screen, the lens and all the bits he didn't consciously understand, finally the box whirred and his digital camera was born.

'That's better.' Tim started snapping away. He took a picture of each board and a couple of the study. He also took a shot of Clarice Crowfield's large portrait and the shrine to her past. After a minute or so he felt he had enough.

'Timothy,' Phil whispered. 'I propose a noble

retreat now. We can take our findings to Inspector Kane.'

'Not yet. There was a door under the stairs,' Dee said. 'Maybe that's a passage to the basement? We should check there first – what if they *are* keeping him here?'

'She's right.'

The monkey let out a deliberately dramatic sigh. 'Fine, but let us be quick and, above all, silent.'

In one motion Tim picked up his rucksack from the floor and swung it on to his back. As he did so, the bag connected with a mug that was on the corner of the desk. They had been so cautious, *so quiet*, up until this moment.

Helplessly all three of them saw the china cup fly through the air, twirling and reflecting the dim light of the study. There was nothing they could do but watch as it fell to the hard, stone floor. It smashed with a tremendous amount of noise, sending shards of china sliding and spinning across the ground.

'Oh, deary me,' Phil said. 'I suspect this shan't end well.'

Chapter 17

Crowfield House seemed to thump awake with commotion above them. Tim and Dee ran towards the exit but heard feet already on the stairs.

Someone was coming.

Tim slammed his back against the bookshelf, behind the study door. There was no room for Dee who spun round once, twice, looking for a place to hide. She hit the ground, and rolled under the desk, getting out of sight just as Clarice Crowfield stormed in holding a baseball bat. Her face was half asleep, but her body was wide awake. Long black hair hung down, unusually neat for someone who had been asleep moments ago. Tim stood in the shadow of the door, watching her crouch and pick up a shard of the mug.

'I know you're still here,' she yelled, still with her back to where Tim was hiding. He could see Dee's panic-stricken face pinned down on the other side of the room. The monkey had burrowed as deep as possible into Tim's shirt pocket – the tiny heart beating rapidly on his chest.

Clarice looked up to the desk where the mug once was and then stalked towards the window. Like a suspicious dog, she smelled the air. This woman was even worse in the flesh than in Stephen's memories – seeing her made this whole break-in altogether more real. Too real in fact. Tim guessed that the woman, crazed from head to toe, would have no problems using that bat. He hastily gestured Dee to come out, but she looked behind her at Clarice standing right there, facing away, and frantically shook her head. Then she waved Tim off, silently mouthing for *him* to run. To go and get help. Maybe she was right, maybe that was his only option.

When Clarice inspected the opening to the secret passage, Tim edged his way around the door, holding his breath until it began to hurt. He saw her thin arm squeeze the bat, then he leant round to look into the hall: the coast was clear. Staying low, he darted out through the front door, leaving it wide open in his haste. He knew this was going to make a noise and could already hear Clarice shouting for Stephen, and the sound of someone tearing down the stairs.

Tim ran as fast as his legs would carry him on to the driveway, skidding to the ground and hiding behind Stephen's black car. Lying on his front, he perched on his elbows by the back wheel, Phil hanging his furry head out of Tim's top pocket. From here he could see Clarice – still clutching the weapon – and Stephen coming out, searching.

'Dee's still in there,' Phil whispered.

'Yeah, I know. We've got to go and get help.' Tim would be returning in good time, with Inspector Kane as support. 'Soon as they've gone back inside, we'll make a break for it.'

Blinking through the morning sun, Stephen scanned the front drive, sweeping his gaze backwards and forwards across the huge expanse of land surrounding the building. Then he slowly began walking towards the car – towards Tim.

'Oh no,' Tim said, looking around for somewhere to go. He crawled further, reaching up to one of the back doors, hoping hard that it was unlocked.

'Got ya,' Stephen shouted as he leapt round to the side of the vehicle, but there was no one there. Standing up straight, he sighed.

Tim had got in the car, just in time. On the back seat he lay as still as he could, only a metre away from Stephen, who was searching the bushes nearby. And then, in the footwell, Tim spotted a camera with a telescopic lens and a familiar green cap.

'Can you see anyone?' Clarice yelled. 'Stephen!'

'No, Mother.' His voice echoed. 'I'm going to have a drive around the grounds, see if I can find anything.'

No, no, no, Tim thought to himself, burying his face in his hands.

The driver's door opened and Stephen climbed in. Curled up in a ball on the back seat, Tim tensed every muscle. If Stephen looked up at the mirror, or behind him, that would be it – game over. But instead he patted his dressing gown's pocket and then climbed back out. No keys, Tim thought.

Phil clambered up on to the top of the seat. 'Timothy, we have got to think of something. We have got to figure something out. A solution, better than a jetpack,' the monkey said. He began literally jumping up and down in panic. 'He's coming, Timothy, he's coming back!'

But Tim was already in the front seat, the imagination box open next to him.

'What are you doing?' Phil asked, his voice quivering. 'Timothy? Have you ever driven before?'

'I have sat in a go-kart,' Tim replied as he lowered the handbrake down and looked at the steering wheel in front of him. 'Once.' He pushed the key he'd just created into the ignition.

'So . . . no then.'

'I suppose not. Phil, come here. You have to direct me – I can't see over the dashboard.'

'This seems to be a dangerous idea.'

'Yes, it is, but unless you've got a better one . . .'

Tim reached up and adjusted the inside mirror. Stephen was almost upon them.

'Go!' Phil yelled as he leapt into the front.

The car rumbled into life and Tim rammed the stick into 'Drive', relieved that it was an automatic. Stephen stopped a little behind, seemingly bewildered that it had started – he looked at his own keys and frowned. The vehicle pulled away with spinning wheels – gravel and mud flung up around him.

'OK, Phil, which way?' Tim asked.

The monkey was clinging on to the dashboard, inches from the windscreen. 'Right,' he said. 'Turn right.'

The car gently swayed *left*, its wheels getting caught on the grass. It jolted and bounced off the tarmac, slowing dramatically.

'The other right!' Phil yelled.

Tim remembered the walk up to the house, he guessed the gate was perhaps three hundred metres away. Getting back on to the road and straightening the tyres, he pushed the accelerator pedal, gently pulled the steering wheel round, feeling the speed increase. Faster and faster. He couldn't see anything at all – he had to trust the directions.

'More right,' the monkey said. 'Less right. Less right.'

'So left?' Tim screamed.

'No. Less right.'

'Less right is left!'

'No, it isn't.'

Two wheels were on the road, two were on the grass. Again they had slowed, and Stephen grabbed the back door and managed to get it open. Tim looked round, swerving as he did so. Stephen stumbled and lost his grip. They swung up on to the grass and then, without Phil's directions, he pulled it back towards the long driveway.

'OK,' Phil said. 'Good, now a tiny bit right, then a bit more, then a bit more.'

'Your directions are confusing,' Tim shouted. He took his foot off the accelerator and knelt up to look out the windscreen, seeing the curve of the drive all the way down to the large iron gate.

'Quick,' Phil yelled.

Tim's foot slammed on to the pedal as Stephen threw his body at the back of the car, bouncing the suspension, but he slipped and went tumbling over and over on the road. They weaved, picking up more and more speed as they approached the gate – Tim knew he'd have to hit it with quite some force to go through.

'Left a bit, left a bit,' Phil said, pointing at their small target. He then began screaming. They sped closer and closer, the revs still lifting.

Tim, eyes shut, grabbed the wheel and braced himself.

They smashed through the gate, sending the cast iron scraping across its roof. Birds erupted from nearby foliage. Bricks and lumps of metal spun in the air as the car screeched on to the road, scattering debris everywhere.

'We did it,' Phil yelled.

'Now where?'

'Keep going, it's pretty straight.'

They drove for a while. Tim checked the mirror to see they weren't being followed. Behind them was the entrance, utterly destroyed, and further back,

Crowfield House, still proud on top of the hill. They approached a lay-by and Tim slowly pulled in, with careful directions. They toyed with the idea of driving all the way to the police station but, with adrenaline fading, decided against it.

'I can't believe it,' Tim said. 'We made it. We made it without crashing. Well, apart from the crash. No *accidental* crashes though.'

They were still rolling when Phil jumped down on to the seat.

'Counterfeiting money, burglary, car theft, trespassing ... any other crimes you feel like doing today, Timothy?'

'Hey, I didn't steal anything from inside the house – take back burglary.'

'I think it counts, you still broke in.'

'*We* broke in Phil. Quite successfully too. And the getaway went well I think.'

'With my directions and your expertise, we are unstoppable. We should do rally driving.' Phil said.

'I know! A very, very successful first drive. Well done, team.'

'Hang on a second,' Phil looked over his shoulder, then down at the seat. 'We are still moving.'

The front wheels hit the mud of the deep ditch at the edge of the road and the bonnet disappeared down, thumping into the dirt.

Tim was flung forward, caught by his seat belt, Phil landed on the cracked windscreen. The imagination box bounced and ended up hanging by a strap off the top of the passenger seat. The car was stuck, almost vertically, in the base of the trench.

'Handbrake,' Tim groaned. 'Well ... I'm sure he has insurance. We've probably done him a favour.'

They quickly clambered out and ran into the woods as the warm sunrise burst through the trees – long columns of light came between branches, making glitter of the morning dew. But there was no time to appreciate it – they had to head down the hill, into town, to the police station, to tell Inspector Kane what they'd found. And they had to be fast. Dee was still trapped inside the house, completely at the mercy of the Crowfields.

Chapter 18

Tim was out of breath when he arrived at the back of the police station. He'd jogged all the way here, down the hill, through Pine Common and across Glassbridge. It took well over an hour, his pace slowed by exhaustion. Throughout the whole journey he'd been anticipating the look on Inspector Kane's face when he showed him these pictures, told him about the memories they'd seen on the computer. *You want hard evidence? Well here it is.*

On the way Phil had suggested Tim create a phone, which he did, but despite repeated attempts they couldn't get a signal. Assuming he wasn't making things properly because of stress or tiredness, Tim blamed himself for the failing.

Then, to vent his frustration, he'd thrown the mobile at a tree.

Reaching the police station, he swung his legs over a low metal barrier in the car park and crossed the tarmac to an alleyway at the side of the building leading to the front and to the main entrance.

'Phil, inside, we're nearly there,' Tim said, stepping over a small bag of rubbish. The monkey disappeared inside his shirt pocket.

Just as they arrived on to the street Tim was surprised to hear Elisa's voice. He shot back into the alley and slammed himself against the bricks, then squatted down behind a large bin. She was crying. He heard Chris's voice, which was strange because he was meant to be away on business.

'But why isn't he taking it more seriously?' she said through tears. Chris hugged her tight. They were standing right in front of the station door. 'I don't care what he says, I'm *sure* this has something to do with Eisenstone.'

'It's fine. Like he was saying, kids usually turn up safe,' Chris said. 'You never ran away when you were young?'

'No, never. Where would they go?'

'Let's get home, all right? Tim might have already come back.'

'OK,' she sniffed.

'Besides, breakfast is in full swing and those waitresses aren't going to shout at themselves. The hotel can't run without its backbone.'

'I don't care about the hotel,' she said.

They walked past the mouth of the alleyway, Chris with his arm round Elisa. Tim leant back behind the bin, deep in the shadow, so they didn't see him.

'Timothy,' Phil said.

'Shh!' he wrapped his hand over his pocket.

Phil struggled and mumbled as he tried to break free. 'Mmmtimm, Tim,' he released his grip. 'Why are you hiding? Go and speak to Elisa, let her know you are OK.'

'No.'

'Why not? She was crying.'

'She ... she'll be fine. Look, we ran away, a huge breach of the rules. I'm going to be in *massive* trouble. Once I've delivered the camera and fixed all of this, then we'll face the music.'

'Timothy, I feel you are being quite unreasonable. If you gave her more of a chance, you would see that she just wants what is best for you.'

'Phil ...' he sighed, lifting the monkey from his pocket and placing him on the bin's lid. They were eye to eye. 'If she sees me now she'll be furious. You don't know what she can be like, she'll—'

'If you explain it to her, she will be able to help—'

'I don't need help,' Tim said, feeling an odd mix of emotions after Elisa's tears. He'd never seen her that upset – he was surprised to see sadness, not anger. 'I've been by myself long enough now, and it's fine,' he added, with a shrug. 'I don't need her ... I don't need anyone.'

'Timothy,' Phil said, very deliberately. 'If that is true ... then ... why did you create me?'

And, right there in that alleyway, Tim stopped and nodded, realising that maybe, just maybe, he wasn't OK with being alone.

'That's a sound point, little monkey,' he said. 'A sound point.'

Tim held his shirt pocket open and he leapt back in.

'Let us sort this pickle out,' Phil said, looking up. 'Once and for all.'

Inside Glassbridge police station, Tim walked right past the receptionist, who'd clearly only just arrived for work. 'Um, excuse me,' she said behind him, flustering with her handbag, but he just kept going. Inspector Kane's office door banged open.

Thankfully, despite the early hour, the policeman was sitting at his desk, sipping coffee and flicking through the newspaper. The page was open on the travel supplement, photos of exotic islands stretched across the page in vivid colour. He lifted his head.

'Listen, I've got something to show you,' Tim said.

'Um, good morning?' Kane closed the paper.

Tim pulled out his digital camera and threw it to Kane.

'Look at the pictures on there,' Tim said. 'Dee's at Crowfield House. Pretty sure Professor Eisenstone is too. You've got to help them.'

Inspector Kane held the camera – he was being

infuriatingly slow. 'You look very tired, Tim. You getting enough sleep?'

'No, not really. Been up all night. Plus there's this sort of demon monster that crawls through the vents in the Dawn Star. Really scary thing. Please, look at those photos.'

'Ah, I see. When I was young it was under my bed. Every night I'd get my mother to check. I was convinced there was a clown or something down there, your imagination can sometimes play tricks on you.'

'Can't it just?'

Inspector Kane spent a few moments pressing buttons. He frowned as he flicked from one incriminating photo to another.

'These were taken in the study of Crowfield House,' Tim explained. 'Clarice Crowfield married Professor Eisenstone's former partner, Professor Bernard Whitelock, before he died. I believe Clarice and Stephen Crowfield, the Dawn Star's new chef, have kidnapped Eisenstone and are keeping him somewhere.'

Clearing his throat, the policeman looked uncomfortable.

'And Dee is still there, still at Crowfield House,' Tim added. 'You've got to go there and fix this.'

'I'll hold on to this for future reference. We'll see how it develops,' Kane said. He opened his top drawer and placed the camera inside.

'What?' Tim said, bewildered. 'You're not going to arrest them? Aren't you listening?'

'Tim, please lower your voice,' the policeman whispered, glancing to the door. 'I've just returned from Crowfield House myself – you could be in very big trouble.'

Tim frowned. 'Why were *you* there?'

'Why?' Kane coughed. 'They called me about a break-in. I could arrest *you* for trespassing. Now, this is your last chance. Just *go home*.'

'But, the pictures. They've taken him. The longer we sit around here, doing nothing—'

'Tim, Tim, Tim. You've explained, very broadly, your theory. Well done, good work . . . but you haven't explored motive. *Why* would they want Eisenstone? Why kidnap him?'

Taking a long breath in, Tim tried to calm himself.

He gave a lot of thought to his next words. Weighing up the pros and cons and having considered all the scenarios, he finally decided, for the first time in a while, to be open and honest. It was the only option left, the only way to make Kane take what he was saying seriously.

'Because of the importance of his work,' Tim said.

'What does that mean? What do you know about his work?' Inspector Kane was leaning forwards, speaking with another layer of worry in his voice.

'I know more than anyone else. I know more than his own daughter. I probably know more than Stephen and his scary mother Clarice. And I certainly know more than *you*.'

Screwing up his eyes, Kane cupped his face in his hand.

'Tim,' he said, slowly shaking his head, 'I told you to leave it, didn't I? I said it would be trouble if you carried on, but you didn't listen. I warned you.'

'Inspector Kane, do *you* know what Eisenstone was working on?' Tim said, undoing the zip on his bag.

'I know a fair bit about quantum physics. I read some of his book—'

Tim laughed. He looked across the desk – his eyes were drawn to a very posh pen.

'That's a lovely pen, isn't it?' he said.

There was a moment of silence. Kane seemed confused by the change of subject.

'Yes, yes it is. My ex-wife gave it to me. She bought it in Chile.'

'Did she?' Tim said. 'Quite rare, is it?'

'I don't know if it's rare, but they don't make them in this country. Special wood. Plus, my name is engraved on the side . . . anniversary gift.'

'Strikes me as quite a coincidence that I have one too,' Tim said, reaching in his bag and pulling out a pen identical to Kane's. 'Strange that.' He threw it on to the desk and sat back in silence.

The inspector saw that it was exactly the same as his own – same material, same tiny font spelling his name. He lifted his head. 'Where . . . where did you get this?'

'I made it. I made it in something called an

imagination box. *That* is what Eisenstone was working on. A machine that creates anything you can imagine from the ground up, atom by atom. Things like a sausage, a jetpack, a nightmare and even a self-aware, miniature monkey who is perhaps more articulate than I am.'

Tim then pulled out the device and put it on the desk. The cube, sleek and silver, greeted Inspector Kane's eyes. The question mark on the side was facing him – he admired the craftsmanship. Then, slowly, he shook his head again – this time in awe.

'Where did you get *that*?'

'You want to know where I got it? I made it. I made it in Eisenstone's machine. I made my *own* imagination box.'

'That's impossible.'

'Well, actually,' Tim pointed at the device on the desk, 'no it isn't. Listen, I think the people who have taken Eisenstone want to make their own version of this. I saw a *huge* prototype in a secret lab in their house. You have to help me. It's not too late to save him.'

Kane looked, for some reason, as though he had just been delivered some sad news. 'Tim ... I ...'

'We've got to go to Crowfield House,' Tim said.

'Yes,' the policeman replied, standing, sighing, and looking down at his feet. 'I think you're right.'

Glassbridge police station's underground car park smelled of damp concrete and exhaust fumes. A pipe dripped nearby. Kane looked over his shoulder, as though to check no one was around, then opened the back door of his car. Tim eased his rucksack off, about to climb in, but without saying a word, the policeman snatched it from him. Tim was more confused than worried at first.

'Get in,' Kane said. 'Now.' When Tim hesitated, wondering why he seemed so firm, the inspector grabbed him by the arm. 'I said, *get in*.'

'Wait,' Tim said, realising something was wrong. He tugged away but, before he could get completely free, the policeman picked him up and threw him over his shoulder. As he did so, Phil went flying out of his top pocket, landing on the tarmac behind. The monkey quickly scurried out of sight under the car, as Tim was bundled into the back seat.

A moment later, the wheels screeched and they pulled up the ramp on to the road. He listened to Kane's muffled voice as he made a phone call in the front seat – he was repeating what Tim had told him at the station. At the end of the conversation, he said, 'Yes, you need to get rid of everything, and I want the rest of my payment today – the pressure ... it is mounting. I want every penny. I need to be gone. Then we're done. All right, Clarice, see you in ten.'

There it was, there was the answer to their question – this was why Kane had been so reluctant to investigate: he was working with the Crowfields. Tim silently cursed himself for being so *foolish*. For getting carried away, for not stopping to think. Feeling terribly alone, he grabbed his chest, holding the space where Phil should have been. The monkey was by himself now, in that car park, and Tim wished hard he wouldn't stray any further from home.

And so Inspector Kane did as Tim asked and took him back to Crowfield House, but for all the wrong reasons.

Chapter 19

When they arrived, Kane took Tim by the shoulder and shoved him firmly through the front door into Crowfield House's hallway. It looked different in broad daylight, somehow grander. Tim felt hopeless, unarmed, without his imagination box. The corrupt policeman had hold of it the whole time.

He turned and tried to push past, but Kane was too big and heavy to move out of the way. Without speaking, the inspector pulled him by his collar and dragged him into the study. He stumbled inside. In front of him, by the desk, Stephen and Clarice Crowfield were waiting. The young chef averted his eyes, perhaps ashamed of what he'd done, while Clarice casually inspected her fingernails.

Tim worried about Dee – had she got out? Had she managed to escape like him? He felt a twist in his stomach, terrible guilt – he had left her, left her to get help . . . only to return with just the opposite.

'Ah, our little intruder,' Clarice said, with a clap.

The police officer silently held out Tim's imagination box – he watched on in horror as it fell into Clarice's skinny hands. In turn she passed over a duffel bag and then Kane, the one man Tim thought could help him, looked down at the floor, sighed to himself and left with his payment slung over his shoulder. Clarice pulled the contraption straight from the rucksack and burst out laughing, a crazed cackle echoing around the high-ceilinged study.

'You?' she said. 'You've made it work? All the secrets, all we need, wrapped up tightly in your tiny little skull.' Clarice leant down and grabbed Tim by the cheeks. 'Would you like to show us how your atomic constructor works, Tim?'

'No, not really,' he replied. 'And it's called an imagination box.'

'That's . . . that's actually a nice name,' Clarice said.

'That's much better. Stephen, why didn't *you* think of that?'

Her son stepped forwards. 'Why don't we dismantle the box to see if—'

'Stephen, you tapeworm's tapeworm.' Clarice tensed her jaw, without turning. 'When I want your input, I'll ask for it.'

'Right,' Tim said. 'You guys are absolute fruit loops. Crackers. That's obvious. But, come on, this is getting out of hand – you need to grow up. Where's Eisenstone?' Tim was testing the water – he was still unsure exactly what these guys were capable of. Perhaps he could talk his way out of here?

'Eisenstone?' Clarice frowned.

'Yes, I know you kidnapped him,' Tim added. 'Let us both go and I'll show you how the imagination box works. I'll even teach you to use it. That's what you want, isn't it?'

Clarice clapped her hands and swung her head back. Her features looked distorted when she smiled. Behind, above the desk, her portrait seemed a different woman. Tim imagined she was once quite pretty, but now it was as though all the colour was gone from her.

'I love this boy,' she squealed, all teeth and gums. 'Trying to buy his way out. How endearingly optimistic.' She knelt down in front of him and ruffled his hat, oblivious to it being an integral part of his imagination box. 'You, my young boy, are in no position to bargain with us.'

'What do you want from me?' Tim asked, pulling away.

'If you actually have a working atomic— imagination box, then we'll need to take it apart for answers.'

'Take it, it's yours,' Tim said.

'Still trying, bless.' She tilted her head. 'You broke my favourite mug, my gate and you crashed Stephen's car. I'm afraid it's just not an option for you to leave here intact. Loose ends, you understand.'

Clarice clicked her fingers and Stephen stepped forwards and grabbed Tim's arm. He struggled and tugged away.

'I'm sorry,' Stephen said.

'No, let go,' Tim yelled. 'Get off. Get off!'

As Clarice approached, clutching a black bag, he kicked and twisted his body. She slammed it on his head, plunging him into darkness. Then he felt himself being carried. He thrust and wiggled for some time until he realised it was no use. After a while, he was dropped on the ground and he heard a door slam behind him. It was bolted shut before he got the cloth off. Rattling the handle proved useless.

Dark, dingy and smelly – this place was a fitting home for a prisoner. After a while his eyes adjusted – gradually he saw more and more. There was a mattress on the floor and the door had a small window with three vertical bars.

A figure sat, hunched over, in the corner.

'Hello?' Tim whispered.

'Tim? Tim! Is that you?' the professor said, stepping forwards from the shadows.

'Eisenstone?' Tim ran and hugged him tight.

'Yes, yes, I'm so very happy and so very . . . so very sad to see you. Indeed. Why on earth are you here?'

'It's a long story. But I've found you, I've finally found you. I knew something was wrong. I knew you wouldn't go without saying goodbye. You left your watch at the hotel. I went full detective.'

The fact that he was now in as much trouble as the professor didn't dampen his burst of happiness. However, he quickly came back down to reality when he thought of Phil and Dee.

'Oh yes, yes, yes, the watch. Yes. Tim, yes I did. I've been in this terrible, terrible place the whole time. But why are you here, in this cell?'

'I'm sorry. I told Inspector Kane all about the imagination box. I thought if he knew, it would make him more likely to find you. I didn't realise he was part of the scheme. I mean it's just so . . . unprofessional. I've gone right off him after all this.'

'Yes,' Eisenstone said. 'Indeed, quite the snake.'

They both sat on the edge of the mattress, on the floor. Tim realised he had to come clean about what he'd done in the lab that day when the professor left him alone.

'You made *what*?'

'I created my own imagination box,' Tim explained. 'Wished for more wishes.'

Eisenstone was flabbergasted. 'And ... indeed ... I mean, does it work?'

'Most of the time, yeah. Can be a bit inconsistent, but on the whole it's good. Plus, look, the reader is actually just a woollen hat.' Tim passed him the black beanie.

'Astonishing.'

After he'd put it back on his head, he explained everything he'd done since they'd parted ways.

'All by yourself? Quite amazing.'

'I wasn't ... I wasn't by myself ... Dee helped.'

'What? Why?' Eisenstone had terror in his voice. 'Where is she now?'

'Not sure ... last time I saw her she was hiding under the desk upstairs.' Tim nervously scratched his scalp. 'To be honest, I've made a bit of a mess out of all this. Not quite as clever as I thought I was.'

'Oh,' Eisenstone sighed, worn by fear. 'I suspect if they'd caught her, she'd be in here with us. Let's take comfort in her absence. Indeed.'

'Yes ... I'm sure she's fine,' Tim said, despite not being sure at all. 'We saw their giant imagination box upstairs, their reader . . . what are they planning?'

'Clarice . . . she . . . I think she wants to take credit for it. She's hell-bent on making it work. I shudder to think what she intends to create inside.'

'And the teleporter? We saw that too. Is that Whitelock's?'

'Yes, yes. I only saw it briefly, but I'm fairly certain that's the one he built.'

'So, how come it's here? You said someone burned his lab and stole it. Was it her? His own wife? She killed him?'

'It . . . it seems so. I was never introduced to Clarice, but I heard on the grapevine he'd met someone. Perhaps this was her plan all along. Maybe that's why she married him. We'd grown distant, Whitelock and I . . . He was a different man. There was an . . . an incident and he was, shall we say, in a vulnerable state of mind . . . But I still can't see how he could marry such a woman. But I suppose he was . . . in love.'

Tim wanted to press the professor further about his old partner, about why they had drifted apart, about what had actually happened between them. It felt as though there were things Eisenstone was not sharing. But the subject seemed to upset him.

'So,' Tim said, 'they've been trying to read your mind, right? To find out how the box works? We saw an empty folder on their laptop in the lab.'

'That's right, yes, indeed. I've managed to resist it so far, managed to take my thoughts elsewhere.'

'Right, I know it's a big secret and everything. I understand the technology can be misused, wrong hands, got to be safe, I get all that, but were you not tempted to just tell her?'

'No. Because then she'd come after *you*,' the professor said. 'Your mind – your imagination – that's where their answers lie.'

Tim smiled at the thought of Eisenstone protecting him. 'Well, I'm here now. Is there some kind of deal we could come up with? A compromise?'

'Ah, no, no. Tim. No, sadly that won't work. It is imperative, crucial and essential that we escape. I really can't overstate that. Indeed, yes, yes. We *must* escape. You see, when they are finished with us, once they've made their imagination box work, they are going to put us in the teleporter.'

'To go where?' Tim asked.

'Nowhere.'

'Um?'

'Oh my, yes. Remember I explained how a teleporter works? We will in fact disappear from the first teleportation chamber, but they'll ensure we never arrive in the one next to it. Deconstructed but not reconstructed. Wiped, as it were, off the face of the earth.'

'Hmm,' Tim said. 'Doesn't that seem a little ... insane? Clarice is off the chart.'

Eisenstone nodded.

'So, fine, escape it is ... how?' Tim said.

'Where's Phil?' the professor asked. 'He's quite small, nimble. He could help.'

Wishing once again for the monkey's safety, Tim explained that he'd fallen from his pocket in the car park.

'Ah, a shame indeed. Right, OK. They've got *your* imagination box. It's only a matter of time before they take it apart. Oh yes. We need a plan. Come on Tim, get your thinking cap on.'

'OK, right, the door is locked, that's obvious . . . Wait, what . . . that's it,' Tim stood up.

'Well . . . I . . . yes . . .?'

'Get my thinking cap on.'

'Well, indeed.'

'I've got it on! I'm wearing my hat. The reader. I can use it from here. I can make something right now . . . Something that can save us . . . Something that can defeat them . . . Hmmm . . .' Tim thought quietly for a moment. 'There. Done. Now . . . we wait.'

About ten seconds later, there was an almighty roar from upstairs. 'BEEEEES!' Stephen shouted, his voice thundering through the vast building. 'Very angry bees!'

Tim had, in actual fact, created robo-bees – cybernetic insects programmed to attack everyone upstairs and then fly down to the basement and etch away at the door with their miniature drill-stings. As he'd hoped, a few of the tiny silver things arrived – their buzz sounded digital as they started work on the concrete around the hinges, a tidy pile of dust beneath them.

They were a good inch through when Clarice stomped down to the cell.

'Oh no, you don't,' she said as she bashed them to death in the darkened hall. 'Tim. That was pretty smart,' she huffed through the bars, straightening her hair. 'It was incredibly dangerous – I could have been stung. However, I managed to lock Stephen in the lab to deal with them. Anyway, I need that hat. I assume it is the reader. Yes? The reader for your box?'

'Nope,' Tim said from the darkness. 'Just a regular old hat.'

Clarice tapped on the bars. 'Come on, cough it up.'

Tim turned to Eisenstone, who gave him a quick nod, so he removed the reader and passed it through the hatch. Clarice's fingers, five little twigs, waited and then snatched it.

'A mobile reader … very, very clever,' she said, turning it over to look. 'Thank you, Tim. Goodbye. For now.'

Later, in the fain, grey light of their prison, Tim stood up and walked from one wall to the other, pressing against each. 'There must be a way out, there must be.'

The lock at the end of the corridor clanked open and footsteps came towards the cell.

'That's Stephen,' Eisenstone quickly whispered. 'This is our only chance. Indeed, I think if we catch him in the right mood he might let his guard down.'

Tim nodded. The professor held his index finger up to his lips. Stephen's profile could be made out through the bars.

'Food,' he said.

The hatch opened and two bowls of lukewarm porridge were pushed in.

'Nice trick, kid,' Stephen said.

'Oh, the bees? I am sorry. I didn't want you to get stung.'

'Well, I did. Lots.'

'Look, listen,' Tim said. 'What are you doing? You're going to be in just as much trouble as your mother. I know it's not your fault, but the police won't know that. You can't take the blame for what she does. You've got to let us out of here.'

'No. I can't. I can't. Mother . . . she will . . .'

'Indeed, yes, we'll make it look like we escaped by ourselves,' Eisenstone added.

Stephen fidgeted and checked up the corridor. 'Right, OK,' he whispered. 'I'll come back—'

'STEPHEN!' a voice bellowed from upstairs.

'I'm sorry, I'm sorry, I have to go. I'm sorry.' He disappeared up the hall, the door at the end clunked and, with its lingering echo, he was gone.

Suddenly, one of the bowls of porridge exploded, splattering sloppy oats on the floor and up the wall. Frantically gasping for air, Phil tried to get the thick food off his face as he clambered out.

'Ah!' he wheezed, clutching his tiny throat. 'Ah, air! Precious, beautiful oxygen.'

'You're here,' Tim said. 'You little hero.'

'I hid . . . hid in the . . . porridge . . . I nearly . . . I almost drowned . . . in porridge,' Phil groaned. 'That is *not* how I wish to die.'

'You came for me,' Tim said.

'Really, it is no problem . . .' Phil's voice was croaky. 'My pleasure.'

'How did you get here?'

'Mostly . . . rooftops, telegraph wires. I am quite the climber it seems. Then I snuck in the house through a . . . a cracked window frame.'

'You were upstairs? Did you see Dee?'

'I am afraid to admit I did not. Let us hope that she managed to get away safe and sound.'

'Yes, yes, yes. Good. This is good,' Eisenstone said, thinking. 'Indeed, yes. This might just be our ticket out of here. If you can sneak up there, oh yes, Phil, we may very well be able to . . . escape.'

The monkey, being small enough, planned to make his way upstairs, where he'd steal the keys to the cell and bring them down. Their last hope, their last chance, went through the bars with the odd oat still clinging to his fur.

'Good luck, Phil,' Tim said.

'See you soon, chaps.'

However, not two minutes after the monkey left, Clarice and Stephen arrived. She had a wheelchair and he was holding a length of rope.

'We're ready,' she said, opening the cell.

Chapter 20

Stephen had handcuffed Eisenstone to the old-fashioned wheelchair and Clarice tugged Tim along by the scruff of his shirt. They approached the bookshelf in the corner of the study, the secret entrance to the lab. Across the room, Tim spotted Phil, poised on the desk, leaning from behind the antique lamp. True to his word, he held a set of keys in his tiny paws. Tim shrugged helplessly as they went through the passage behind the books, stepping over countless dead metal bees strung across the floor.

Once inside the cold, gloomy lab, Tim's eyes locked on to his imagination box – it was intact on the side of one of the worktables, but his reader hat had been changed. They'd put wires in it and it was now attached to *their* reader.

'Tim, come here,' Clarice said, pulling him closer.

'What are you doing?' he asked, glancing up at their huge steel machine.

'Not that it's any of your business, but having inspected your imagination box, it seems hardware really is not our problem,' Clarice said, fiddling with an exposed circuit board. 'In fact, our device is perfect. The issue is software. The problem is our minds. Our imaginations. That's why Professor Eisenstone couldn't make his work either. Not until *you* showed up. Perhaps it's because you're a child. Perhaps you're a genius. Who knows?'

Tim couldn't help but feel a little bit proud again – he liked being the only one able to make the invention work, even if he didn't fully understand why. 'But what have you done with my reader?' he asked.

'We've wired it up to ours. Two readers, one atomic constructor— Imagination box. Now the only thing left to do is to use your head to make it work.'

Clarice leant forwards, 'Then I'll know for sure if mine is built correctly.'

Clarice stepped back and begun untangling the cables connecting the readers.

'Wait,' Tim said. 'So you're going to get me to imagine things for you?'

'No,' she sighed, as though he was being stupid. 'I'm going to imagine something, then my reader is going to send that thought into your brain, then into my box. We're using you as a signal transmitter, nothing more.'

'Well, no. I refuse,' he said, with a shrug.

'You know what, Tim,' she whispered, 'I was sort of hoping you'd say that. Stephen!' she yelled.

Her son flicked a switch and the other end of the large laboratory lit up, a bright white beam throwing shadows across the floor. Tim saw the teleporter, the two tall chambers. In the left hand one was a person – she was frowning behind the glass.

'Dee,' Eisenstone shouted. 'No!'

'Now,' Clarice said, picking up a small control panel. 'I press this button and it's bye bye. Poof. Gone. So why not just do exactly as I say, yeah?'

'Why?' Tim said, looking over to Dee, who silently tutted, rolling her eyes inside. 'Why are you doing this?'

'Why?!' Clarice narrowed her eyes, as though she was insulted by the question. 'Do you know who I am?'

Tim shook his head. 'Haven't a clue.'

'*Exactly*,' she said. 'I was going to be the prime minister one day. That's what they said. I was on my way up. Can you imagine what it feels like to have everyone know your name, to be voted in by the people, to represent all the residents of Glassbridge, your neighbours, your friends, your family – only to then disappear, to become a *nobody*?' She turned to Stephen. 'To have your career cruelly curtailed by a screaming, whining little baby?'

'So you're going to pretend *you* invented the imagination box?'

'Pretend?' she laughed. 'Look at what I've achieved. This is *real*. My name will go down in history.'

'OK ... I think I get it. Your methods are a little iffy, morally,' Tim said. 'But I get it.'

'Oh, young man, judge me by my *results*.'

'And, plus, I don't know *that* much about politics,' he said, lifting an eyebrow. 'But I was under the impression there were easier ways of gaining some popularity?'

'You'd think so, wouldn't you?' she said. 'You'd think your dear husband wouldn't be completely helpless, useless, unable to make *anything* work.'

'Bernard Whitelock,' Eisenstone said, his head hanging, tears brewing, utterly defeated. 'You married my best friend and then you killed him. All for what? For this? To get his technology, to exploit him for his inventions?'

'Oh, but you've got it so ... so wrong. He wasn't your friend, remember, not after what you did ... And, besides, I didn't kill him – just the opposite. I gave him everything he needed ... Isn't that right, Bernie?'

Eisenstone's gaze slowly lifted as a figure stepped from the side of their huge imagination box. Tim recognised the old man from the photo he'd seen – hunched, his eyes flashing in the darkness.

'Bernard . . . but . . . you're . . .' The professor's voice was shuddering, as though they were looking at a ghost.

Perhaps they were, Tim thought, as Professor Whitelock limped towards them, alive in the shadows.

Chapter 21

'But ... but ... you're dead,' Eisenstone said, his eyes darting, searching for answers.

'Well, he's not, is he?' Clarice mocked. 'Are you not paying attention?'

'The lab ... it was burned down –' the professor squinted at his old friend – 'You –'

Silently, Tim waited for further explanation – he was just as confused.

'Smoke and mirrors,' Clarice said. 'It was my idea, wasn't it, Bernie? I thought the best way to finance the research was to cash in his life insurance. It'd mean he couldn't leave the house – he'd have to work here, all day every day. Little did I know that Bernie was *hopeless* ... We tried and we tried but still, we couldn't make our imagination box work.'

'So you resorted to dirty tactics indeed.' Eisenstone glanced at his trapped granddaughter.

'Well, nice guys finish last,' she added. 'We tried softly, softly – Stephen stole your briefcase, even broke into your house once again to look for more notes. But when we heard you were leaving the country, there was only one thing for it. Kidnapping you was just a means to an end – don't take it too personally. Mind you, after what *you* did to him, wiping you off the face of the earth seems a reasonable punishment.'

Professor Whitelock was fiddling with their reader – connected by countless cables to Tim's – yet it was obvious from his body language that he didn't like Clarice's words. Tim wondered what she meant – that was the second time she'd accused Eisenstone of doing something to his former partner.

Dee's muffled banging caught his attention.

'I . . . I don't understand,' Tim said, looking down the long room at the metal chambers, all bright under the spotlights. 'Why the imagination box? I mean, if you can make a teleporter work—'

'It doesn't work,' Whitelock snapped over his shoulder, through clenched teeth. 'It never makes the subject reappear. It can break things apart but it can't put them back together again. It's *never* worked.'

'Well,' Clarice said. 'It certainly fulfils *my* needs.' She wiggled the controls with a maniac's smile.

'Why is it so easy to destroy, and yet so difficult to create?' Whitelock whispered to himself.

Clarice twirled in the middle of the lab, surrounded by her victims. 'Isn't it just wonderful what we have achieved together,' she said, glancing around. 'A device up here –' she pointed at their imagination box – 'meant to bring things into the world, and at the other end of the spectrum –' she swung herself round, facing their teleporter – 'a device to remove them from it.'

Tim then spotted something small on the tile floor, peering from under one of the worktables. It was Phil – he lifted a tiny finger to his lips. Looking quickly away, Tim hoped no one else would clock him.

Whitelock thumbed a switch on the fixed panel

next to their imagination box and there was a loud, deep thud, followed by the familiar electric whoosh, like an old vacuum cleaner powering down. A few bulbs on top of the device flickered, glowing through the mass of electronics near the high ceiling.

'It's on,' he said.

The tall machine dwarfed Tim. It was about the size of his bedroom and had windows, with thick rusted bolts around the edge and a walk-in door at the front. Clarice stepped towards the contraption. She took a moment to peer inside, placing her hand on the glass. The excitement was all over her face. Not for the first time, Tim felt rhythmic surges of anxiety. The only feasible hope left was Phil. For now, Tim would just have to play along.

'Perhaps,' she said, crouching to pick up their hefty reader, 'it'd be best if Bernie tested it first ...' She passed it to Whitelock.

Clarice then pushed Tim's hat on his head, and fiddled with a plug by his ear. Whitelock approached, now wearing their reader. Face to face, they stood, connected to one another by lengths of different-coloured wire that hung between them like they were pylons. Tim's reader was, in turn, linked up to their imagination box.

'Remember,' Clarice added. 'Bernie will imagine something, it'll go through your noggin and then to the machine, so make sure you relax.'

Tim shuddered from a slight tingling on his scalp, like the prickle of static electricity, as they began transmitting via his mind. Gradually, thoughts and images infected his brain; he could observe what Whitelock was thinking. He could sense his memories, see his past and feel his emotions.

Sickened, Tim clutched his hat and began pulling it off. Clarice, standing behind, slapped her hands on top, holding it in place. The experience was so overwhelming he could no longer see the room. Tim's entire consciousness was being hijacked. Thunder drummed in his head, followed by what sounded like a harsh, rising wind.

*

When he opened his eyes there was absolute

silence and he was in a different place. He could see notes, paperwork and an old computer. There was daylight coming from a window. He looked down at his hands – he was an adult. Although conscious, he couldn't control his movements – he was merely an observer.

A noise caught his attention. He turned to see Eisenstone. But he looked younger with brown hair and fewer wrinkles. They were in a different lab. It was a little like a hospital with white surfaces and expensive equipment.

'Let's just do it,' Tim said, but his voice was different. He was Whitelock. He was reliving a memory and could sense that this was years in the past.

Nearby was what looked like a dentist's chair. Through Whitelock's eyes Tim could see a reader. But it was different, it was giant – like a dome hairdryer – and it had its own stand and its own control box larger than the main part of the contraption. There were warning stickers up the side, one sporting what Tim recognised as the symbol for radioactivity.

Whitelock sat down in the chair, looking up at the

technology above his head. There was a loud electrical buzz, like the hiss of television static. He was excited – it was actually going to work. He was sure.

'You don't have to do this,' Eisenstone said as he attached sticky pads to Whitelock's temples. 'I want this to happen as much as you . . . but . . .'

'George, full power,' Whitelock replied, looking him straight in the eye. 'Let's just get it done. Let's make history.'

'Indeed,' Eisenstone said, now smiling. He checked his silver pocket watch.

Then, Tim noticed the letters 'TDACD' printed on the side of what looked like a very early prototype of the imagination box. Although he didn't know why, he was acutely aware that what they were doing was dangerous.

Eisenstone placed his finger on a large red button housed on a control box near the arm of the chair. As he counted down from ten, Whitelock closed his eyes.

'. . . three . . . two . . . one.'

Click.

There was that roaring wind again. Agony tore

241

through him, every vein swelled, bone seemed to bend. Tim could feel every moment of it. There was screaming, deep, guttural. It sounded distant, then he realised it was coming out of his mouth.

A flash of hands, twisted in spasm.

Time stuttered and leapt forwards. Lying on the floor, he could see the ceiling, blurry and spinning. The room was red with a rotating light above, whipping round and round. An alarm.

'Are you all right?' a voice asked, muffled, like an overheard phone conversation. He turned to see Eisenstone crouched next to him looking terrified. 'Can you hear me? Are you all right?'

All at once, Tim knew what they'd done. He could sense that this day, this memory he was seeing, was the last time Professor Eisenstone and Professor Whitelock had worked together. Something went wrong, terribly wrong, with the experiment. The reader had been too powerful and it had somehow damaged Whitelock's brain.

It had changed him.

The two professors, partners, had then gone their

separate ways. Tim felt the ache of a lost friendship. Whitelock spent years alone, obsessively working on his teleporter and on a new imagination box. Speaking to no one, he kept himself to himself. He laboured, day and night, but couldn't make either machine work.

Tim now realised why Eisenstone had looked saddened, even ashamed, whenever the topic of his former partner arose. All these years he had blamed himself for what happened – for the failed experiment. But Whitelock had insisted on being the guinea pig, he knew the dangers.

The memories continued to flow into Tim – he now saw Clarice before she married Whitelock. She whispered in his ear. 'Professor Eisenstone used you, he *used* you. He didn't care about the risks.'

'But,' Tim said, in Whitelock's voice, 'I insisted. It was my choice.'

'No,' she went on. 'He only cared about himself. Stay here. Stay here and we can get back at him *together*. We can be the first to make the atomic constructor work. We'll win. We'll beat him.'

Clarice was nice to Whitelock at first. She helped

him, loved him. Then she convinced him to fake his own death – she said it was the only way he'd be able to finance his work. He agreed. He did everything she told him to.

Tim relived a rushed wedding, a hatched plan – fire engulfed Whitelock's past, sending shadows jutting across his future. They moved his imagination box and his teleporter into Crowfield House, which became his home, his place of work and then, eventually, his prison.

'Tell him I'm sorry,' a faint voice said. Tim realised this was aimed at him. Whitelock was sharing his thoughts. 'Tell him it isn't his fault – what happened that day, in the lab. He shouldn't blame himself. He doesn't need to feel guilty. It's not his fault. It's not his fault. It's not—'

'—working,' another voice interrupted. 'It's not working. You're not trying hard enough. Give it here.'

Like a jolt from a nightmare, Tim was yanked back to the real world. His vision refocused, like looking through water at first and then bursting above the surface and seeing clearly. It had seemed like a dream – it felt as though hours had past, but they'd been wearing the readers for less than a minute.

Clarice had tugged the device from her husband's head. Tim and Whitelock stared in silence at one another. Initially he had thought what he'd seen was merely the jumbled contents of an old man's mind. But somehow he felt these memories had been recalled deliberately – as though Whitelock wanted someone else to see the truth.

'Let me have a go,' she said. 'It seems safe enough.'

Across the lab, Tim saw Phil had scurried up to the teleporter and was tugging at the handle. He decided that the moment the monkey got it open, the very second Dee was out, he was going to make a break for Eisenstone's chair, and then for the door. They might all be able to escape this madness.

Chapter 22

Clarice Crowfield smiled – all her features distorted – as she lowered the large metal reader on to her head. Her long black hair was flattened, hiding much of her face. She looked truly mad.

'Right,' she said, leaning close, eyes wide. 'Let's try this properly, shall we? You ready, Tim? *Let's create something.*'

At the other end of the laboratory, Phil was still silently battling with the teleporter door. Tim knew that if he refused, Clarice could still obliterate Dee with the flick of a switch. Perhaps, he decided, helping her make something could buy them some time. It could open the window for an escape.

'Fine,' Tim said. 'Let's do it.'

Stephen, Whitelock and Eisenstone all watched on.

The two readers, connected to one another, began whirring. Although Tim *really* didn't want to see inside *her* mind, he decided to submit and allowed it to happen. Steadily, once again, thoughts that weren't his own travelled down the wires and infected his brain.

The contents of her psyche arrived all at once, in a big, timeless batch – the lab disappeared, his eyes rolled back. He felt darkness, loneliness, failure, anger. And then he saw fire – thick, swirling flames bellowing out of a building.

Finally, through the frantic flashes of insanity, something began to form – a shiny gold ingot, rotating slowly on a pedestal. This is what Clarice was imagining, he reasoned. Everything else he had seen just slipped through the net.

The gold bar was clear – Tim could see it vividly. Just as he did with his imagination box, he envisaged all the finer details. But the image flickered, fizzed, as though a conflicting signal had arrived. Clarice simply couldn't focus, couldn't filter out the pollution.

And then Tim felt something terrible, something uglier than he could ever have imagined.

From the abyss of her mind arose a low, haunting sound. Breathing. Something was there, something hidden in the emptiness. Her demon, waiting in the void. Distant gurgling, getting closer, louder until it became clear, until the madness, the hatred, was right there, right in front of him.

Tim could feel it, he could hear it, he could *see* it. Something that should never, ever exist in the real world. Then he became aware that the thought was travelling from his brain, down the cable to the vast imagination box in front of him.

He yanked his reader off – the real world flooded in around him – and slammed it on the floor. It was too late. The damage had been done. He took steps back, almost falling as he retreated. Eisenstone looked confused by the fear.

Tim shook his head, tears in his eyes.

The machine drummed into life, like an orchestra hitting its climax. It flurried with all sorts of noises as mad flashes of light – blue, green, yellow, red, red,

red – shot into the room. Tim looked up at Clarice, who was watching in awe. The dance of her eyes was like the composer's hand – up and down, left and right – commanding the sounds. Whitelock and Stephen too, stared on. Even Eisenstone was amazed to see it working, despite his concern.

The contraption strained hard, steam shot from the vents, wires glowed, as it constructed *something* from Clarice's mind. Eisenstone gradually started edging his wheelchair backwards with his feet, copying Tim's retreat.

'What's . . . in there?' Stephen asked.

A brutal thud echoed around the lab. Then another. Dust and brick crumbs fell from the ceiling. Light bulbs wobbled, sending shadows dancing. Everyone took a step back. Then another thump, the loudest yet. Circuits buzzed and the lab fell back into silence.

An explosion ripped the front of the chamber open as a monster smashed out with ease. Sparks, shrapnel and a cloud of smoke hailed its arrival. It broke its way free, growling over the twisted metal of the imagination box.

This was the embodiment of madness, of hate, of the darkness within Clarice. The creature stood like a gorilla, only it was huge, larger than an elephant – its back pressed on the high ceiling. Its flesh was red, covered in open sores. Half its body was bold and imposing, the other half looked lame and unfinished. And its face – there was no animal on earth that it resembled. It was simply a monster. No visible eyes, just hollow cavities. Clear, sloppy, drool dangled from its mouth. Razor-sharp teeth poked out, some breaking through the skin. Its head bobbed up and down as it heaved deep breaths, vapour shooting with each exhalation. Like a lion, its throat rumbled as it took in its new environment.

No one in the room knew what to do. No one knew what to expect. For the first time Tim tore his gaze away to see Eisenstone, who looked as though he was about to faint. Clarice too looked terrified – perhaps also wondering where her gold was.

The demon bellowed its war cry and leant inches from her face, sending her hair swirling. It then heaved its body up into the air and slammed a fist down towards Clarice, who leapt backwards as the floor spewed up from the impact.

'Oh my word,' Phil said from Dee's shoulder, now by Tim's side.

She grabbed his arm. He flinched. 'Tim,' Dee said, 'I think we should leave now.'

The monkey had got her out, and, it seemed, just in the nick of time.

Tim nodded. 'That's a good idea.'

As the monster swung its heavy arm to the left, smashing a gaping hole in the wall, everyone burst into action. Eisenstone pushed himself back, slowly tilted in his chair and then fell to the floor, still tied up. Grunting with every movement, it thundered towards Clarice and Stephen, who quickly turned and ran their separate ways. Tim ducked behind the creature to the table and grabbed a set of keys, then his imagination box and his reader. With his hands full, he returned to the professor – Dee was already on him, tugging and pulling, trying to get him back on his wheels.

Tim fumbled with the keys as they watched the

monster lurch for Stephen, who leapt over one of the lab tables and crouched behind. The beast's arm pushed into the wall above him, crumbling bricks as though they were sand.

Its attention then turned to Clarice. She picked up a stool and threw it. The wood shattered against its face. It didn't even react – rather it advanced, destroying everything in its path.

She fell into one of the teleporter's chambers, the one Dee had left open, and sealed the door. Just as it lifted itself, about to destroy her, another stool bounced off its side.

Stephen looked as though he regretted throwing it as the demon's head snapped round to him. It stomped sideways now, annihilating the table he was hidden behind in two strikes of its heavy claws. Splinters and rubble stood in a dusty pile where Stephen had been. A pipe had broken and water squirted out into the lab, splashing on the animal's shoulder.

As Dee finally got Eisenstone's cuffs off, Tim saw Stephen crawling, scrabbling away to the other side of the room, where Whitelock was hiding.

Now it slowly turned again, to face Eisenstone, Dee and Tim.

They frantically untied the leg ropes as the monster ploughed forwards. It picked up a hefty lab table and flung it spinning through the air as the professor stood, free from his restraints. All three of them dived in different directions – rolling over to see the wheelchair gone, smashed to pieces against the wall.

Led now by Eisenstone, Tim and Dee ran towards the door, ducking another of the creature's swipes. This separated them slightly and, before Tim could catch up, he was struck and knocked from his feet, skidding and bouncing like a rag doll, across the floor and thumping to a stop against the warped metal of the broken machine. Then, without a beat, a supporting beam from above fell in front of him, followed by a mountain of bricks so high he could no longer see the others.

His legs were trapped. As he tried to free them he heard a curious, loud *conk* and felt a sharp ache on the top of his skull – a chunky piece of concrete landed by his side. It must have hit him, he thought, oddly relaxed. There was a faint taste of blood in his mouth and a hiss in his ears as his vision tunneled and then faded smoothly to black.

Chapter 23

The lab was calm. Things had started to settle, everything was becoming still. Tim blinked awake and touched a tender lump on his head. Still dazed, he watched Stephen crawl out from his hiding place. Everything was a blur – it all played out like a fever dream.

There was a distant banging, but Tim was still too dizzy to process it.

The destruction was extreme. The imagination box was in pieces and piles of rubble sat on the floor beneath tall holes in the walls. Sunlight beamed in. It was a surreal thing to see. The laboratory seemed like a ruin from an ancient civilisation – completely transformed in the short attack.

Tim watched Whitelock limp out of one of the new openings, off into the garden. He didn't look back.

The thumping continued and Tim heard a faint voice.

To his right, at the other end of the lab, he saw Clarice locked inside the teleporter. She was hitting her fists on the inside of the window, yelling at the top of her voice. It sounded as though she was under water.

Stephen looked up through the bright light, suspended, almost solid in the cloudy air.

'Let me out!' Clarice shouted, softened inside the teleportation chamber. 'Open this up, Stephen. Open it!'

He strolled towards his mother and gently grabbed the handle.

'Quickly,' she said.

But, with a deliberate tug, he snapped it off, locking her inside.

'Stephen? Stephen. Open this up now. You ungrateful little tick. You will open it.' She pushed her hands against the glass, exposing her teeth. 'I know you will.'

Casually, purposefully, Stephen picked up the controls. He placed his thumb on the button.

'Stephen Crowfield,' she screamed. 'You are a disgraceful, ghastly, repugnant lump of—'

He flicked the switch. Light flashed from the teleporter. Clarice fizzled and dissolved in an instant. Teleported to nowhere. Deconstructed but not reconstructed. Every atom, every particle that made her was now separated.

Clarice Crowfield was gone.

Stephen showed no remorse. Rather, his shoulders fell backwards and his chin tilted up. Smiling, he turned and clambered out through the wall. He landed on the lawn, and escaped towards the trees at the back of the house.

Now alone, Tim wondered whether Stephen had been waiting his whole life for such an opportunity. Would he have done it if he'd known he was being watched? There was no way to be sure.

After he'd cleared the debris from his legs, Tim

scrambled to his feet and made it outside. When there was no sign of Eisenstone, Dee or Phil, he went back in through the front door, finding them in the study.

'Tim!' Dee yelled. 'You made it out. It's in there, in the passage to the lab.'

Phil dived from her shoulder and slid straight down into his shirt pocket. Tim quickly explained what he'd seen, but there was no time to discuss it. The secret bookcase was shut – Eisenstone had tipped a tall, wooden clock on its side and rammed it against the door.

'We need to keep it contained,' he said over his shoulder. 'Indeed, you two grab the desk – we need to trap it.'

'What's going on?' a voice asked. They all whipped around to see Inspector Kane.

Eisenstone grabbed Tim's arm and shuffled him round behind himself, then did the same with his granddaughter.

'Yes, yes, what do you want?' he asked.

Kane held his hands up. 'No, I'm … I'm sorry.

I changed my mind. I don't want the money. It was wrong. I came back to rescue you.'

The professor squinted, unsure whether to trust him or not.

'We don't need your help,' Tim said.

'Yeah, jog on, Kane, you're not our friend,' Dee added.

'Look, it doesn't matter now, listen, listen, listen, we've got to get out of here,' Eisenstone said. 'There's a . . . it's a . . . a monster, indeed, yes, in there. We've got to go.'

'A monster?' Kane laughed. 'Sorry?'

He curiously approached the secret entrance.

'No, no, no. Really, stay back. Seriously,' Eisenstone said.

The case vibrated, books rattled off the shelves. Below, the floor rumbled and above the chandelier clinked and wobbled. Kane took a few steps back.

Before he could say another word the cabinets exploded into a thousand pieces. The beast appeared. Eisenstone, Tim and Dee went for the door as fast as they could. Looking back, Tim saw Kane hold his ground.

'Stop, police!' he shouted.

With a husky grunt, it tilted its head, as though contemplating the order. But then it snatched Kane by the legs, swung him round and threw him the full length of the room. He crashed straight through the window, disappearing from sight.

'Oh deary me,' Phil whispered.

Behind them the creature began taking the study to pieces, like a toddler flinging toys in a tantrum. It made short work of the broad antique desk, rolling it over, sliding it across the floor and then catapulting it over its shoulder. It ran its claws across the wooden shelves, turning them to wreckage with ease.

Everything it could see, it destroyed.

Tim, Eisenstone and Dee all made it through the front door and outside. They stopped on the drive and turned back to the building as a desperate roar made birds flee from nearby trees.

'What now?' Tim said, catching his breath.

'Right, indeed, it mustn't get out,' Eisenstone replied. 'So long as it stays in there, we should be quite fine.'

The side of the house gave way. It burst through and thudded on to the grass – a torrent of dusty debris and glass followed it.

Clarice's prized portrait landed on the ground amid it all. Her proudest moment, beautifully immortalised in the painting. The eyes looked towards the sky, at the mercy of the surrounding destruction. A moment later, the monster's heavy foot slammed down on top of the picture and twisted purposefully into the mud, crushing it like a finished cigarette.

It turned around and lumbered towards them.

'Back into the house!' Eisenstone yelled. He was right, there was no way they could outrun it on flat ground.

They made it inside, grabbing the door as its face smashed against the wood on the other side, dislodging the grand stone wall. The professor used his back and tried to push the door closed – Dee and Tim too put their weight into it. Snarling breath blasted through the gap and after a struggle the deadbolt clacked shut.

It sounded as though it had retreated.

'It's getting a run-up,' Dee shouted. They all sprinted towards the kitchen. Close behind, it broke in, destroying the doorway, the stairwell and everything it passed through.

They only just made it to the back door in time, charging outside once more. The monster came into the kitchen, twirling and obliterating. The building was collapsing behind it. Tonnes and tonnes of rubble fell, pinning the creature's lower half. It writhed and cried, flinging bricks, pots and pans with every struggle. Its mouth stretched out and tore through the cooker. The pipe split. Gas spewed out, filling the kitchen, making the air wobble like transparent jelly.

The storey above had almost entirely collapsed, turning the ground floor into a kind of pit. Walls stood with a hollow space in the middle, where the creature had trapped itself – upstairs furniture sliding, falling, smashing.

Crowfield House was in ruins.

On the grass at the back, Tim had an idea – he neatened his hat and closed his eyes. A few moments later, he opened the imagination box on the lawn, to reveal a small orange distress flare. Someone would need to light it and throw it into the gas.

Without saying a word, Phil clambered out of his pocket. He took it under his arm and headed back towards the building. Everyone else moved further away.

They watched the monkey scurry up the twisted trellis and climb over the split walls to the tilting roof. From there he could see through all the floors, down to the kitchen. The demon was still struggling wildly, but with every movement Crowfield House tightened its grip.

Phil held the flare upright; it was twice as big as him. With both of his hands he tugged the tag to light it, teetering on a floorboard from the loft that jutted out at a strange angle. Below, the creature threw concrete off its back and stumbled into a space, shouldering against the wall, stirring the gas. It was almost entirely free when Phil finally fired up the flare. It fizzed and sparkled hot, painting him red. From the ground Tim watched the bright glow appear on the corner of the house.

One final, defiant roar.

'Toodles,' Phil said as he dropped it.

As it fell he leapt outwards, towards the grass. Tim watched the flare and the monkey descend in different directions, almost in a perfect reflection of each other. Before Phil hit the ground the stick made its way into the heart of the gas leak. It clattered off a shard of tile and landed.

Fire, light and heat burst out, all struggling to escape the quickest. The explosion was immense. The shock wave hit them like the front of a hurricane – they shielded their faces as the mushroom cloud rose, curving in on itself.

Tim's eyes scanned the grass, desperate to see Phil. Pieces rained down, but the monkey was nowhere to be seen.

'Phil?' he said, stepping towards the burning ruins, the dust now all around them.

Eisenstone grabbed his shoulder, holding him back. 'Don't go any closer.'

'Phil!' Tim yelled. 'Where is he?'

Dee covered her mouth, looking on. The professor

too seemed worried as seconds passed and the monkey still didn't emerge.

The sound of sirens drew nearer. At the front of the house, through the broken gate, a fire engine and three police cars arrived. Their lights flickered blue but their noise grew silent as Tim stared at what was left of Crowfield House.

The building buckled and collapsed further as flames spiralled. A thick mass of black smoke flowed up, speckled and glowing, leaving a long shadow over the gardens. On top of the hill, it would be seen from miles away, filling the sky.

Tim sat on the ground and his chin began to tremble. Phil was in there somewhere. Warm tears fell from his cheeks.

Blinking, Tim thought he saw a shape on the grass. It moved, and moved some more. Then a tiny monkey emerged, limping towards them. Tim stood, ran and skidded on his knees. His fur was blackened and his paw injured, but he was alive.

'Phil!' Tim shouted as he picked him up.

Dee and Eisenstone stood over them. 'Oh yes, yes,

well done little monkey,' the professor said, crouching, the fire reflecting in his glasses.

'What a strange day,' Dee said.

'*Indeed.*'

'That monster tried to *kill* Clarice,' Tim said. 'Her own creation, the first thing she made, wanted to destroy her.' They stood and watched the burning wreckage for a moment.

'I wonder,' the monkey added, 'what a psychiatrist would say about that?'

Chapter 24

Tim, Dee and Eisenstone gave what proved to be long, complex statements at the police station. The officer conducting the interviews spent a lot of time rubbing his forehead and asking them to repeat themselves. Some men in suits also arrived and quizzed them on all that took place at Crowfield House.

All cleaned up and back at the Dawn Star, Tim took the imagination box from his bag and placed the reader inside. Closing the lid he carried the device to his wardrobe and put it on one of the shelves, on top of some old board games. His finger ran over the large black question mark on the side, with a tap on the dot.

Smiling, he shut the door.

Later, he was propped up in bed, with Phil in the

top drawer next to him and Elisa sitting by his side. It took hours for her to stop asking questions, which was fair enough. Tim answered them as best he could but if it wasn't for a talking monkey backing up his claims, she'd have found believing the entire story quite difficult.

After a long chat, Tim settled down into his pillow and, even though he was completely and utterly exhausted, his mind still buzzed with the day's events.

'Sweet dreams,' Elisa said, flicking the light switch off as she left.

No more than three seconds later and the trap against the vent hissed quietly as it was edged out a little, and then slipped off on to the floor. Tim's nightmarish creation was in the room, on the carpet – covered in fresh foam, which wasn't quite as effective as he had imagined. Somehow, the creature's terrifically awful existence had slipped his mind.

He sat bolt upright in bed, staring at what he thought he had just heard. A shadow, something moving towards him.

'Elisa,' he finally screamed. 'Elisa!'

The door swung open and the light flashed on. She stormed fearlessly towards the monster, grabbing it by one of its legs and holding it up at arm's length. It wiggled, writhed and snapped at her.

'Did you make this?' she asked, frowning and raising the corner of her top lip.

'Yes, by accident,' Tim replied.

'It's a funny thing, isn't it?' She lifted it higher to get a good look at its body. It snarled and hissed. 'What does it even do?'

Tim considered this. Now that he thought about it, he didn't know what the beast was going to do when it caught him. Maybe that was why it had never actually attacked, just followed him around. It wasn't the feeling of being hurt that frightened him in the nightmare, nor being eaten or anything like that – it was just being chased, just being . . . *alone*. Seeing Elisa hold it in such a casual way made the creature seem somehow ridiculous.

'Shall I get rid of it?' she asked.

'Yes please.'

'Maybe I'll take it to the zoo in the morning. See what they think.'

'Good idea.'

'Right,' she said, holding the weighty creature far from herself as it had one last screech. 'Goodnight again.'

And, just like that, Elisa took the fear away.

Tim touched the top of his head to double-check he wasn't wearing his hat. Finally, he lay still and felt safe. His imagination relaxed and sleep, *real sleep*, gradually took him.

Epilogue

A couple of weeks later, Tim was sitting in the lobby, his hand swaying left to right as he sketched a human brain. Although he could have created this drawing instantly with the imagination box, there was still something satisfying about the time and effort required to do it the old-fashioned way. Sometimes the fun is in the journey, not the destination, he thought to himself.

Donald Pinkman's time at the hotel had drawn to a close. Near the front door the consultant bid farewell to fellow staff, then finally stepped over to Tim.

'That's very good,' Donald said, nodding at the sketch pad. 'Well, I'm off.'

'All right.' Tim smiled. 'See ya. Oh, and I'm sorry for accusing you of kidnapping Eisenstone.'

'You did what now?'

'It was my mistake. Coincidences, eh?' It had turned out that Donald really *had* just wanted to protect the hotel's reputation.

Bewildered, Donald paused and then had one last stab at an authoritative tone. 'Didn't Elisa say you shouldn't draw in the lobby – messy fingerprints on the sofa . . .?'

'OK,' Tim said. 'Bye then.'

That evening, Elisa, Chris, Tim and Phil went to a science seminar at Glassbridge's large, grand theatre. There was a series of lectures hosted by prominent professors and academics. The headline slot was Professor Eisenstone who, according to the programme, would speak about the exciting advances in 'quantum nanoscience'.

Eisenstone's daughter, Sarah, was there with her husband. Dee was too, wearing her polka-dot dress and the hairband Tim had made. They all sat along the same row and watched excitedly as the professor took to the stage.

It was obvious he was nervous, lit brightly in front of royal-red curtains. A cube-shaped prop by his side was hidden by a purple velvet sheet.

He approached the microphone and began to speak. 'There is a box,' he said. 'Anything you imagine will appear inside. You have one go, one chance to create *anything* you want. What would you pick?'

In broad terms he explained, thanks to some 'incredible technology', that this might one day be a reality. However, he said that it was still 'many years away'. Dee and Tim shared a knowing glance at this – they weren't surprised by Eisenstone's decision not to share *exactly* what had happened over the past few weeks.

Nonetheless, the audience was visibly excited, especially when he revealed a mocked-up prototype.

After the seminar, the professor invited Elisa, Chris and Tim back to his house for dinner. He was cooking at the barbecue when they arrived in the large garden, already populated by Dee and her parents.

'Ah! Yes, yes, indeed yes. My guest of honour,' the professor said, pointing his cooking tongs to the sky.

He took his apron off and came to greet them. 'Tim, let me show you around.'

As they walked away from everyone else, Tim glanced back, slightly concerned to see Chris rubbing his hands and approaching the barbecue.

'He is going to destroy dinner,' Tim said. 'It's as simple as that.'

They headed a little further past the flower beds. Eisenstone was in a jubilant mood, still animated by the presentation. 'I think it went well, yes, indeed.'

'People seemed interested,' Tim said.

'It's . . . it's been a rocky road. How have you been since . . .?'

Tim knew what he meant. 'It was weird having someone else's thoughts in my brain. Odd dreams and stuff but, you know, I'll live.' He looked at his feet, nervous asking about what he'd seen. 'What happened . . . that day . . . in the lab, with you and Whitelock . . . It was . . .'

The professor seemed to know the topic was about to come up – he put on a brave face to explain. 'Yes. Indeed,' he said. 'Now you know . . . you see, well, some of the earlier readers were a little . . . dodgy. The imagination box has been an idea for a long time but it's only recently become what you might call "stable". Back then, it was really new ground, oh yes, we had no real idea what we were doing. The old readers used radiation, like an X-ray of the brain. After that day, after that failed test, Whitelock, well, he was never the same again.'

'I felt that.'

'Yes. He was always keen to experiment on himself. There was always something about him, a part of his mind that made him *obsessed* with progress. But progress at *any cost*. It's quite hard to understand really.'

'No it isn't. I get it,' Tim said. 'He believed scientific advancement was more important than anything else.'

Eisenstone slowed a little, looking warily at Tim. 'That's exactly it,' he said. 'You sound just like him. Anyway, we drifted apart after that failed test. I assumed he blamed me for what happened, for the damage to his mind. I know I've always blamed myself.'

'It's not your fault,' Tim said. 'He wanted to do it. I saw the memory. He was happy to risk anything to make it work. And later Clarice just took advantage of him. He was a victim of her, and of himself – *you* have no reason to feel guilty.'

Eisenstone seemed lightened, as though he'd been waiting years to hear those words. 'Thank you.'

Tim listened to the birds chirping above them, thinking of all that had happened at Crowfield House. Stephen and Kane had been arrested and Whitelock had, once again, gone missing. Of course, Tim had not been surprised to hear that there was absolutely no trace of Clarice.

They rounded a low bush and headed towards the house. Before they made it back to the table the professor stopped.

'I was wrong about the box,' Eisenstone said, almost to himself. 'I told you it could only make concrete things. It just isn't that simple. Indeed. We've seen hate and obsession, we've seen loneliness and fear.' He glanced at Tim's top pocket. 'And we've seen loyalty and love. We scientists occasionally get carried away – indeed, we sometimes think we know more than we do. The imagination box is no different. It's more than a tool, it's more than a toy, it is a bridge, a bridge between our minds and the physical world. We've barely scratched the surface.'

Later on, Tim, Dee and Phil sat together at the back of the lawn near the flowers and tomato plants. Through the trees the orange light painted leopard-print patterns as they idly chatted the evening away.

Tim looked back at the adults, sitting around the table, sipping wine and laughing. He saw Eisenstone pull his silver watch from his pocket to check the time, as Chris cut up a sausage on a plate.

Phil, who had been well behaved most of the day, hidden in Tim's pocket, was now on the ground looking for a clover with four leaves.

'So what, precisely, is it that makes them lucky?' the monkey asked, wading amid the rich turf which was, for him, waist high.

'It's just superstition,' Tim explained. 'Because they are rare, unique.'

The air between them swirled now with the faint

smells of summer: barbecue smoke, fresh pollen and the cool grass beneath.

'At any rate, I think some good fortune would be quite desirable,' the monkey said. 'Perhaps if my search is unsuccessful, which seems terribly probable, you could make me one?'

'Sure,' Tim said. 'If that's what you really want.'

Dee picked up a dandelion and blew gently into the fluffed top. 'It's a strange thing to consider,' she said, squinting through the dancing seeds.

'What is?' Phil asked.

'Having *anything* you want,' Dee said. 'You could see people in the audience earlier – they were all wondering what it'd be. What they would choose. It's an interesting question.'

Right then, Tim caught Elisa's eye – she gave him a comforting smile. 'Yeah, it is,' he whispered.

Glancing around at everyone in the garden – warm and hazy in the last of the day's sun – Tim realised that his answer was relatively simple.

He couldn't imagine needing anything else.

Acknowledgements

A special thanks to my agent Clare Wallace for her support and for making everything happen, to editors Vicki Le Feuvre and Alice Swan for their patience in teaching me all the things I should have already known and, of course, to everyone else working hard behind the scenes.

I'm also indebted to Inge for her love and tea. To Barbara and Mick who help beyond measure. To Christine for giving me my first real job that involved writing words.

And to my hands. Without these this whole thing would have been so much harder. Good old hands.

If you enjoyed reading

The Imagination Box,

you'll love . . .